My Man's Best Friend

A NOVEL BY K. ELLE COLLIER

Printing and binding by Malloy, Ann Arbor MI 48103

Cover art: Tamara Ramsay

Author photo: Ernestine Lona

Cover design, page layout, typography: Erik Jay

ISBN-13: 978-0-9816495-2-8
[$13.95]

Twin Pen Publishing
Studio City CA 91604

ACKNOWLEDGEMENTS

FIRST AND FOREMOST I'D like to thank God, for without Him none of this would be possible.

Well, this has been a long and exciting journey and this book starts a new chapter in my life. There are so many people to thank and I'd just like to say that, if I forget you, please do not hold it against me; I'm new at this, but I will try my best to mention everyone.

To my mom, Yvonne Collier, I love you, thank you for your support and always believing in me. To my brothers Mark, Guy, Lloyd, and Kurt, growing up in a house where it was four to one only made me stronger. I love you guys, and I thank you for your continued love and encouragement.

A special thank you to my twin brother Kurt and your willingness to step in and help me out at that 11th hour.

To Keno Redd, what can I say? You are truly a great friend. Thank you for standing next to me during my entire writing process. Our discussions along with your countless notes and suggestions were invaluable.

To my best friend and sister Kimberly Williams, thank you for your continued support and for loving me unconditionally; stay exactly how you are. To my other best friend, Derrick 'Skiter' (SKEETER?) Jones, your positive energy is infectious; thank you for being a great friend. Ernestine Lona, my photographer and my friend, thanks for your insightful input; tell Frankie I said hey! Kibi Anderson, my sunshine, I love you. Ricky Franck, my Chicago connection, thanks for putting up with me all these years; I'm going to get to Springfield, promise.

Tiffany Brown, one year and counting, thanks for being a great friend. Jonathan Reid, my painting buddy, let's get together and color some canvas. Paul Badger, aka "Leon," we did it. Kristal Clark, thanks for your friendship and the honest feedback, K (pause) bye. Gary Hardwick, my mentor and my friend, let's make this into a movie. Eric Jerome Dickey, the man, thank you for perusing my early pages and encouraging me to continue. Elyce Strong, I appreciate your notes and quick responses; I'm looking forward to your novel. Edwardo Jackson, the self-publishing king, thank you for answering all of my questions without hesitation and putting my mind at ease. Erik Jay, my editor and a really cool guy, thank you for transforming my words into a readable manuscript; don't lose that eclectic personality. Tamara Ramsay, my graphic artist, thank you for seeing my vision and turning it into an amazing cover; you got skills girl, keep holding it down in Barbados.

Shannon Amos, my publicist and my friend. I thank you for believing in me and the success of this book.

Daneen, Dawn, Debbie, and Donna Collier, my four sister in laws, I am blessed to have you in my life. A special thanks to Daneen for your notes and unique insight, I think you have a future.

Leah, Emanuela, Telisha, Brett, Jayne, Deana, Marlon, Tricia, Sonya, Kellie, Brandon, Michael, Judy, Adriane, Ife – you all have touched my life in some way and I appreciate you.

Last but not least, to everyone who buys my book, thank you for your support. I hope you enjoy the ride.

— K. ELLE COLLIER

TABLE OF CONTENTS

1 · YOU WIN SOME AND, WELL... YOU WIN SOME

I KNEW THE MOMENT I laid eyes on Todd Daniels he was going to be my man. My ace, my one and only, hell – maybe even my soul mate. And that's saying a lot coming from me, Kai Edwards, a professional love 'em and leave 'em who never looked back or cared how hard they cried or even how many times they called me a bitch. Didn't matter one bit.

As a matter of fact, it didn't matter at all. You see, my last committed relationship was a whopping three months, the one before that barely two, and the rest – well, let's just say I can count the unfulfilled days using both hands and one perfectly pedicured foot. But Todd was different, he was more than just a man, he was a future, fully equipped with an amazing smile and milk chocolate skin that made you go mmm-hmm. Standing at six feet and a few inches, give or take the small heel on his tastefully black Italian leather loafers. He commanded attention and exuded a certain confidence, which I found help-lessly intoxicating.

I was standing in line at Curt's Coffee House on my regu-lar afternoon break from the office. The coffee house was full of patrons desperately seeking their mid-afternoon java jolt, and I was no different. My caffeine addiction was one of desperation; I found myself almost hallucinating without it. I realized a while ago that I had a dependency, but like I told my mom, I'd rather be addicted to a double latte with soy rather than crack, porn, or even men who cheat on their girlfriends like it was a normal way of life.

I glanced back over to Todd (aka "tall, dark and delicious") and wondered if he was the cheating type, wondered if he left you just as crazy as Glenn Close in Fatal Attraction. Hmm, I think I would take my chances with him.

I scooped up my absurdly overpriced café latte and slowly strolled past him over to a small table for two by the window. He noticed me. Why shouldn't he? I am five-foot six, one hun-dred and thirty-five pounds self with curves in all the right places. I sat down facing Him, making sure He could admire my flawless skin and full lips. I crossed my legs, making sure He could appreciate my smooth yet toned thighs, and my killer calves. Thank you high school track team! I still had his atten-tion as he glanced back not once… but twice. I picked up my latte with my left hand, making sure a bare ring finger was in plain view. Two carats would suffice.

Todd stood about ten feet away from me as he waited for his turn in line. Shifting from side to side with his right hand in the pocket of his well broken in, faded designer jeans, I could tell that he had this certain "thing" about him, this unspoken presence and energy that held my attention. I glanced around the coffee shop and quickly noticed this magnetic presence was holding the attention of two other female admirers, not to men-tion, a male one, as well. No surprise; this brother had a gift of talking without even speaking. As a matter of fact, he was definitely doing a Jedi mind trick on me and every other woman within a twenty-foot radius.

I quickly realized that I needed to up my chances of being the "chosen one," so I slowly crossed and uncrossed my legs as I shifted my body in his direction. I had his attention. I shot him my million-dollar smile. He quickly acknowledged my "come get it while it's hot" gesture. Too bad the woman standing next to him acknowledged it, too. She purposely placed her hand on his back and leaned in to say something to him in an all too familiar way, as she glanced back at me, not so nicely.

Ugh! After seeing the Grinch steal my damn Christmas, I took one last swig of my java, snatched up my purse, and quickly proceeded to the nearest exit. Miss "devil in her blue jeans" watched every step as I made my way out of the café, ensuring that I didn't do a detour into her man's solar system of wonderful.

I stepped outside of the comfort of air conditioning into a thick, affronting wave of the mid-summer afternoon air. It was hot and it was humid. The humidity had a way of setting up residence between my skin and my clothing, pulling them together like a magnet to a piece of metal. I hesitated for a moment, thinking maybe I should go back in, show Miss Thing who had the power – but no, I was already over it. My self preservation mechanism had kicked in, in anticipation of defeat. Instead I took my strides up Randolph Street towards Michigan Avenue. The afternoon rush hour traffic was just starting to thicken. A confluence of sound from the passing of buses, cars, and the nearby L train created a sweet melody of sorts. I took a deep breath and relished in why I love Chicago; the hustle and bustle of the city's downtown is infectious. The varied and unique architecture of the skyline is as diverse as the sea of people ever passing by, Chicago is a big city but yet the occasional smile from a random stranger can make you feel like you are in a small and familiar town. But most importantly, I love Chicago because it is home.

I didn't totally appreciate this great city until I moved to Atlanta right after college, so when my best friend, Simone, called to let me know that her advertising company was looking for a new account rep, I emailed, faxed and damn near FedEx'd my resume to her.

I knew once my resume was in the hands of Simone McCormick, that job at McKenzie and Strong Advertising was as good as mine. Simone was not only my friend, she was my own personal publicist, which for her translated into "I will do just about anything to get my best friend in the same city as moi." Needless to say, three weeks and two days later, I was on my way back home to Chicago to start yet another new life, complete with a great paying job and a plush apartment on the near North Side.

That's one of the many things I loved about Simone. She knew girlfriends were not a luxury, but a necessity – she always like to say, "If you can't count on your girlfriends for good and bad times, who can you count on?" Yep, Simone McCormick made it her mission to show her girls that they were important in her like and I, for one, I appreciated that.

After navigating the sea of business suits, I arrived at my regular newsstand. An abundance of magazines featuring covers of air brushed models, actors and rappers that looked up at me and beckoned me to read, buy and subscribe. I put down my purse and picked up my absolute favorite magazine in the whole wide world, Vanity Fair – well, at least my favorite for this month. Duane "The Rock" Johnson was on the cover. I quickly flipped it open to see a Revlon ad. Halle Berry never looked so good. As usual her skin is flawless, her teeth are perfect and her body is amazing. This is the sister who makes you think of spending your life savings on a face-lift, body wrap, and a ThighMaster. I love her and I hate her.

A movement caught my eye. I looked up to see, Him, Mr. Wonderful from the coffee shop. He was standing less than two feet away from me and looking directly at me.

He stared. I spoke, still looking at the Revlon ad but giving all my attention to him.

"If I'm not mistaken, I think someone is stalking me," I said with a smile.

"Is that right?" Todd said.

"Very much so." I added

"Well in my line of work, that wouldn't be a good thing," he responded.

I slowly closed my Vanity Fair, turned my body toward his while giving him a quick once over – damn he was fine!

"So what type of work would that be?" I asked.

"I'm a lawyer. Divorce lawyer," he said with a half-smile, half-grin.

"Then misdemeanor stalking was probably taught in first year law," I shot back.

"Exactly," Todd said as his smile grew, showing all of his perfectly aligned, pearly white teeth. He extended his hand towards me. "I'm Todd. Todd Daniels."

His hands were big and strong, his voice smooth and hypnotic. I was in awe of this brother, and I didn't know why.

I slid my small hand into his warmth, feeling his roughness in our connection.

"I'm Kai Edwards."

"Nice to meet you – Kai. That's a pretty name. How do you spell it? K-y-e?"

"No, K-a-i."

"Ah, Kai with an 'i,' I like that. Like it a lot."

"Thanks."

"So Kai with an 'i' – do you always flirt with strangers in coffee shops?"

"That depends."

"On?" he asked.

"If you're open to strange women flirting with you while you're with your girlfriend," I answered.

Todd chuckled as he looked from side to side, was he making sure She-Devil was nowhere near?

"That's pretty presumptuous of you, just assuming some-one's my girl."

"Right. So, is she?" I couldn't believe how forward I was being, but if it was going to win me the prize, I had to act quickly.

Todd shifted from left to right, and subtly scanned me up and down as if he were inspecting a used car to buy, looking for flaws that weren't immediately visible to the eye.

"She's a girl who happens to be a friend. So yes, you could say she is a girlfriend," he said as he emphasized "friend" with the lifting of his left eyebrow.

I knew Todd was playing a game of semantics with me and I didn't care. It just made him even more attractive.

"Well, I think Miss Devil in the blue jeans would definitely say she is 'the' girlfriend, the kind entitled to benefits."

"Nope, definitely not benefits."

"You sure?" I questioned.

"Positive. She got the memo," he said.

I laughed; Todd smiled.

"Ah, the memo, but the question is, did she read the memo? Because you see, if she didn't read the memo, that's how miscommunication starts," I continued, "which leads to assumptions, which quickly turn to attachment, taking us back approximately fifteen minutes to the coffee shop when your girl – your 'friend' – shot me a look of death for even thinking about looking in your direction."

"Ah, 'miscommunication' – a very important word in the dynamic of relationships," Todd said.

"Crazy, but true," I added.

"Indeed," he said.

"It's something you should know, being a divorce attorney and all," I said with a smile.

"You have a point. So in the future, I guess I'd better stick to the voicemails."

"Good idea," I said.

We both smiled a bit at our witty, flirtatious banter. We definitely had a connection. And for me, well, that prize was as good as mine.

"So, Kai with an 'i' – is there any way I could get in touch with you to finish our conversation?"

"That depends."

"On?"

"How quickly you send that voicemail."

A bigger smile crawled across Todd's face. "Consider it done," he said with confidence.

We quickly exchanged numbers and a few more lines of flirty banter, gave each other a friendly hug, and said our good-byes. I walked north. Todd walked south, disappearing just as quickly as he had appeared.

I looked at my watch. My five-minute coffee break had turned into a forty-five minute meet-and-greet on Wabash. I took out my phone, hit "Contacts" and the letter "T" and Todd's number came up. I stared at it, wondering if he would really call – but more importantly, I wondered if I would still be interested once he did. I took it all in as I headed back to my office a mere block away.

As the elevators opened to the fifteenth floor offices of McKenzie & Strong, I quickly remembered why I'd left for my five-minute reprieve. Stress hung in the air as I headed towards my office. A big new campaign was starting to take shape and I wanted everything to go perfectly. After settling in, my assistant, Stephanie, buzzed to remind me of a 2:30pm meeting, although that wasn't necessary since Simone was walking through my door before I even had a chance to hang up the phone.

"You're back. Just how long does it take to get a cup of coffee?" Simone plopped down on my plush terra-cotta couch – with green, yellow, and red throw pillows, it was my office focal point and my pride and joy. If it could speak, I would name it.

"I was only gone for fifteen minutes." Although it was closer to forty, why state the obvious? I knew Simone was timing me; she always did, an annoying practice she started in high school.

"More like forty-three minutes." Simone raised an eyebrow as she laid the new campaign art boards on my cocktail table.

Simone and I met freshman year in high school, when her family moved to Chicago from Louisiana. I guess you could call Simone a Creole girl. Her dark brown skin and green eyes were not an everyday sight in Chicago, but go down to the Bayou and there are sistas with those attributes on every corner. Simone and I hit it off instantly. It was like we were born to be best friends, and that's what we became.

So, fast-forward 20 years, and now it's like we were born to be best co-workers at McKenzie & Strong. As far as I was concerned, we were an amazing creative team. Simone and I had been working on landing the "Just B" account for two weeks. Simone has a creative flair like no other, not to mention a hustle that is relentless as well as admirable. "Just B" is the new blue jean line from singer/songwriter Bianca – best described as funky clothes with a spiritual appeal – and I knew we were the women to breathe life into it. Bianca was a free-spirited, soulful singer and her clothing line had to embody just that. So Simone and I came up with a variety of different slogans to go with her name: "Just B love," "Just B peaceful," "Just B creative," and "Just B energy," just to name a few.

Landing this account would definitely get Simone noticed as well as make my stay a lot more comfortable. It was my first assignment since starting the job and I wanted to come out of the gates blazing.

"So what do you think of these babies?" Simone asked, still analyzing the boards. She was always trying to find ways to improve things.

"They're hot as hell! One look and the client will be all over it. I'm not crazy about the model, but the concept is off the hook," I said.

"Oh, the model is just for presentation," Simone said, "let's be clear on that. She will be replaced once the campaign is ours. Right now my main concern is landing this puppy."

"And we will," I said with confidence, just to remind Simone that I had her back 110%.

"I love your positive energy, Kai. Keep that up. We need it around here." Simone glanced at her watch. "We present in an hour. Meet me in my office in 30 so I can brief you."

"I'll be there," I assured her.

Simone scooped up her boards and turned to leave, but quickly swung back around to face me. "By the way, why were you gone so long?"

I let out a huge smile, unable to control any of my facial muscles.

Simone returned my smile with a smirk. "Thought so. Okay, then, what's the brother's name?"

"Todd," I blushed.

"Well, Todd had better be damn fine, keeping you out of the office when we have this project hanging over our heads."

"Oh, he's definitely something to take home for all to see," I said proudly.

"Those are always the best. See you in 30," Simone said, giving me a wink as she left my office.

I leaned back in my chair as I replayed my close encounter with my Mr. Mocha in my mind. I drifted into a fantasy – only to be startled by the ring of my cell phone. I grabbed it off the desk and smiled as it displayed, "call from Todd."

I just loved winning the prize.

2 · UNSPOKEN TRUTH

I CAN'T STOP CRYING.

I try to run but they block my way, pushing me down. Fear has paralyzed me, overcome me, and is running through every inch of my body. I am scared – no, I am terrified. They stand over me, laughing, taunting, teasing. My heart pumps faster and faster, my body is sore and dirty. I look to the left then to the right, plotting my escape. They keep laughing, they high-five each other as if they've done something great, something admirable, but they haven't. I wonder what I've done to deserve this. My mind races, I feel weak, cold, and confused, but they keep laughing, they keep taunting.

"Stop!" I scream over and over until I hear and feel my voice go hoarse.

•

I wakened abruptly from my dream. I heard a buzzer, but

didn't realize it was my front door. I stared into space before making the connection. I slowly sat up trying to focus on the clock – 9:30 am. Perspiration rested lightly on my face, neck, and chest. I ran my fingers through my hair, rubbed my face, wiped the sleep out of my eyes. I felt drained, my body ached. I slid out of bed, grabbed an oversized sweatshirt, slipped it on, and headed for my front door. My hardwood floors were cold to the touch. My legs still ached from my workout two days earlier. Each step was accompanied by small spurts of pain, a bittersweet feeling, one of the tabs I had to pick up for the betterment of my toned body.

I opened the door to see my twin sister, Mila, standing in front of me. By the annoyed look on her face, you would have thought she had been standing there for hours.

"Please don't tell me you were still asleep. It's 9:30 in the morning, Kai," Mila scoffed as she entered my apartment and headed straight to my kitchen.

"Good morning to you, too," I said as I closed the door, shook my head, and followed her.

Having a twin sister definitely meant more attention growing up. Everyone always wanted to know about the twins and we felt like stars in our neighborhood. The fact that Mila and I were fraternal twins gave us our own individuality, not to mention our own styles. We shared the same caramel-colored skin, although her hair was straight as silk while mine was naturally curly. I got my father's height and build, long legs, and athletic body, while Mila was a carbon copy of our mom, equipped with the thick legs, short torso, and big breasts. People always marveled at how different we looked being twins and all, but I had to remind them that we were fraternal twins, not identical.

I entered the kitchen to see Mila preparing a pot of coffee.

"Kai, do you always sleep this late?"

"Mila, I was working late last night and didn't get to bed until about 3am," I said, trying not to sound too irritated that she was breaking my buzzer at 9:30 on a Saturday morning.

"Kai, sleeping late on the weekend only makes it harder to start your work week on Monday."

"And how would you know that? You've never held a 9-to-5 in your life," I said as I removed a bagel from a bag and began slicing it.

"I read it in O magazine," Mila said as if that settled it.

I wasn't going to touch that one.

"So. Why are you here so early?" I asked as I belted out a roaring yawn.

"Did you forget, darlin'? We're going shopping today," Mila said as she started putting away the dishes that had been sitting in the drying rack for three days.

"How could I have forgotten? You reminded me three times yesterday, email, phone, then text."

"I know how forgetful you are, girl."

"No, Mila, now that would be you, which is why you're here now instead of at our agreed upon time of noon."

Mila stopped as she looked up at me.

"Oh dear, you're right, I must have mixed up my schedules somehow. Oh well, since I'm here we should get an early start."

"Mila, does your husband ever wonder why you scurry out the house at the crack of dawn?" I asked. "I mean, most men like to get their 'edge off' in the morning and you, well, you jump ship before Charles even has a chance to pull into the dock."

"For your information, Kai," Mila replied, "Charles and I do have our scheduled time together."

"Scheduled time?"

"Yes," she said. "Scheduled time. It's something we have to do. I mean, between his surgeries and the twins there's really no time for spontaneity in our lives. You'll see, once you get married – that is, if you ever do get married. Speaking of marriage, do you think that will happen in this lifetime?"

"Please don't start, not today." I seethed. Regardless of how sharp I came back on the subject of marriage, it always seemed like Mila heard, "Please, let's talk about it more, much more."

Mila shifted her weight from her left foot to her right as she put her right hand on her hip. "Kai, you're moving into an age bracket where men don't look anymore."

"And what age bracket is that Mila?"

"You know, thirty-five and up, which is right around the corner. Men don't look at you as marriage material, not as much anyway. Basically, your window for bearing them kids is closing at a rapid speed."

"Oh, God, Mila, would you give it a rest, please? I don't give a damn what men think. If I meet a man who truly loves me, it won't matter what age I am. At least I'll know that I married for love and not for money."

Mila stopped and looked at me. I knew that had to have stung. I hated it when she pushed me to say things I shouldn't say. Mila stayed silent.

"Mila, I'm…"

"So what stores do you want to hit first?" Mila blurted, not making eye contact.

"It doesn't matter to me, as long as they sell shoes and purses I'm good," I said, still trying to get Mila to look up at me, but she was hurt.

"Well, that leaves just about every store in town, doesn't it?" Mila quipped as she continued putting my dishes away.

I looked at Mila. She was wearing a silk blouse and A-line skirt, more like she was going to an interview rather than the mall. Mila had always been a lot more conservative than me. Had she pursued a career, any career, my guess is that she would have been a great accountant. On the other hand, I needed anything, as long as it was creative.

Mila continued to busy herself around my kitchen. It was time to shift the conversation.

"So I had another one of my dreams again," I said, trying to make eye contact with my twin.

Mila didn't even acknowledge what had just come outta my mouth.

"Did you hear me?" I asked.

"I heard you Kai, why you telling me?"

"Why not?"

"Well, for starters, I'm not a psychologist."

"But you are my sister."

Mila turned, evading the discussion. She opened another cabinet, sighed, and began putting away more dishes. I took a deep breath as I ran my fingers through my naturally curly hair (that needed a wash and deep conditioner). I walked over and poured myself a cup of coffee, adding my hazelnut coffee creamer and five – yes, five – cubes of sugar. It's amazing that I've never fallen into a diabetic coma. I took a sip and watched Mila continue to organize my already organized cabinets.

"I just thought…"

"Why do you have your plates in the same cabinet with your glasses?" Mila asked, ignoring me completely.

My patience was wearing thin with Mila's anal ways.

"Mila, every time you come over here you rearrange something and then when you leave I can't find shit," I snapped.

"I'll make a chart of where everything is. How does that sound?"

"Sounds stupid," I said. "How about you just leave everything the way it is?"

"Why would I do that? You obviously need someone to come in to organize things for you." Mila paused to pull a large glass container off a shelf. "What is this?"

"What do you think?"

"Oh, my God, a bong?"

"It's a glass candle holder." I snatched it from Mila's judgmental grip and put it back in the cabinet.

Mila scrunched up her face at the sight of the blackened candleholder now sitting back on the shelf.

"Listen, do you want some breakfast? Because I'm starving," I said, staring at the bagel that I just prepared and knowing that I needed something more.

"We should go out to eat," Mila suggested.

"I was going to cook," I said.

"Nonsense, we should go to that cute little café on the corner. What's its name again?"

"Café Bijou," I said.

"Yeah , Café Bijou. You go get decent and I'll finish up out here," Mila said as she quickly turned her attention back to the organized clutter that awaited her in my cabinets.

I gave up. As I headed off to take a shower, all I could think about was how much my sister raked my nerves to no end. Then my mind shifted to Todd and our date later that day. I was nervous about seeing him. For the last two weeks we had been doing the whole "get to know you over the phone" thing – and one night we talked for five hours, as if we were in high schoolers all over again. The only thing that was missing was my mother picking up the downstairs receiver and threatening my life if I didn't hang up immediately and go to sleep.

I wondered if I should tell Mila about my mystery man I met through a chance encounter at a coffee shop. I wondered if I should tell her about how the very thought of him brought butterflies to my stomach. Nah, I thought, I think I will keep my little secret and my butterflies to myself – at least for a little while, at least until after our first date.

3 · RESERVATIONS... FOR TWO

I WAS NERVOUS ABOUT my date with Todd, I didn't know what to wear – more importantly, what shoes I was going to rock. Shoes can definitely make or break an outfit, just ask Sex in the City's Carrie Bradshaw; in addition to Charlotte, Samantha, and Miranda, Carrie's best friends were Marc Jacobs, Jimmy Choo, and Manolo Blahnik.

In my opinion, a good piece of sexy footwear can make any woman look tantalizingly irresistible. On the night of my first date with Todd, I needed to be a one-woman smorgasbord. I sat at my desk contemplating where I should meet Todd for drinks and dinner – he insisted that I pick the place, my favorite place, but the only problem was I had five favorite places. That's part of the beauty and the challenge of Chicago; There are tons of great restaurants, so picking a favorite one was not the easiest task, at least for me. I finally narrowed my options and made the selection of Blackbird on West Randolph. The ambience alone would make it the perfect place for our first date: it was cozy, simple, and very classy, not to mention their American style cuisine was exceptional. I picked up the phone and made a reservation for two at 8pm, leaving enough time to run home to shower and change so I'd get there smelling good – and looking even better.

Simone poked her head in my office; she was on her way to lunch and wanted to know if she could pick me up anything for me. I told her that I was eating light since I had a date. Intrigued, she entered my office.

"Date? Would this date be with that Mr. Wonderful you met the other day at the coffee shop?"

"That it would," I said, confirming with a huge smile.

"Oh, do tell, so where are you crazy kids going tonight?" Simone joked, flopping down on my office couch and kicking up her shoes.

Simone was wearing a fabulous pair of camel leather Jimmy Choo sandals with silver accents, from the new spring line. She's is not one to be caught in an old pair of any style shoe, and by old I mean last season. If Simone could find the real Jimmy Choo she would have his baby, just to guarantee a monthly supply of footwear – not to mention a lifetime of bragging rights.

"I just made reservations at Blackbird," I said.

"Trey nice," Simone replied as she made herself even more comfortable on my couch. "So what are you wearing?"

"Now that, my dear, is the $64,000 question."

"Well, of course, you have to start with the shoes," Simone offered.

"I know, that's why on my way in this morning I stopped over at Bloomie's and picked up these beauties." I pulled out my new Marc Jacobs shoes, metallic gold leather with a slender, black four-inch heel. Simone sat up at attention, looking ready to salute my new addition to the family, as I pulled out the left shoe and swung it around my index finger by the strap, as the scent of new leather wafted through my office. "You like?"

"I like a lot," Simone gushed as she stood up to get a closer view.

She grabbed the right shoe from the box and examined it from all angles. "You have really outdone yourself with these," she said.

"You damn right I did, $580 bucks' worth, but well worth it."

"One look at these," Simone intoned, "and I guarantee he'll skip dinner and drinks and go straight for dessert – which is you, of course."

"That would be nice, but there will be no sex to be had on the first date," I added quickly.

"Oh, are you back to the whole celibate thing again?" she asked. "Because I never understood that, uh, 'way of life,' you know?"

Simone sauntered back over to the couch and sat back down.

"I mean," she said, "would you buy a car before you test drove it, or for that matter buy a tube of lipstick without testing it on the back of your hand? What if he's got some hidden disability you don't know about, that'd be grounds for divorce – and a big settlement, too."

"Hold on, now. I'm not saying I'll wait until we get married," I replied, "just until I really get to know him, that type of thing, and that could be three months or six months. It's kind of a 'new me' kind of thing."

"Mmm-hmm," Simone sighed. "Twenty bucks says you sleep with him tonight."

"Simone!"

"What?"

"Can I get a little bit of support from you?" I asked.

"I'm totally supportive of this new, uh, 'thing' of yours," she added quickly, "but I'm also supportive of winning some easy cash." Simone laughed at her own loopy logic.

"Thanks for the support," I deadpanned.

"Anytime, anytime, that's what best friends are for," Simone said. "Okay, gotta go." As Simone got up to leave my office, I picked up my Marc Jacobs again and wondered if Todd would even notice them.

•

"Nice shoes," Todd said, admiring my fancy footwear for a full five seconds before heading uptown to exam the rest of my wardrobe. My wondering quickly came to an end.

"Thanks," I said with a big smile on my face. As far as I was concerned, my night was already complete; he noticed the shoes. I glanced down to get another look at them myself, and yes, I did good. I'd decided to accent my shoes with a long metallic gold skirt with ruffled pleats and a simple form-fitting, wife-beater tank top, of course, accentuated with three beaded necklaces of all different lengths.

I had to admit, I looked fabulous.

I'd arrived a few minutes early to get a seat at the bar, since Thursday nights were popular at Blackbird and I wasn't about to stand in my new Marc Jacobs for an hour pretending like my feet didn't hurt.

"So what are you drinking tonight?" Todd inquired as he waved down the bartender.

"I'll just have a house Chardonnay," I said.

I'd waited to order a drink until Todd arrived, for a few reasons: one, I hate to drink alone; two, I didn't want to be tipsy when he arrived; and three, I wanted to see if he would order for me. I hate it when a guy invites you to dinner and doesn't buy the first drink.

"So we finally meet again," Todd said as he scanned me once again from my head down to my fabulous toes. "I was starting to forget how you looked."

"Wow, I guess my first impression must really suck!" I exclaimed.

"It could use some work," he joked.

"Cute."

"That you are," Todd said, this time with a more serious, seductive look. I took a sip of my wine and returned his look with my own seductive smile.

"So, how's the food here?" Todd asked.

"It's great, American Cuisine – can't go wrong with that."

"Let's hope not."

There was a pause; one might call it an awkward one. Since this was the first time Todd and I had actually been face-to-face since we first met, I figured we were both just a little nervous. I decided to redirect the conversation a bit.

"So you said on the phone that you were opening up your own law practice. Where is it going to be?"

"Over on West Adams, off State Street. I got a good deal on the office space, so I had to jump on it, not to mention it's close to home."

"That's right, you live near Dearborn Station. How is that area?"

"I love it," Todd said. "You can't go wrong living down-town."

"That you can't," I agreed, even though I preferred the North Side (not as much congestion).

Todd had mentioned in our first meeting that he was from D.C., a Howard undergrad, Northwestern Law, and now a resident of my hometown, Chicago. I was impressed. I like a broth-er with some letters behind his name, especially someone as sexy as Todd.

"So how long have you been living in Chicago?" I asked.

"Well, including law school, five years now."

"And you like it?"

"For now," Todd said with a smile.

"What does that mean?" I inquired.

"Don't get me wrong, Chicago is a great city, but I'm a DC boy. That's where my roots are. I'll eventually move back there, seeing that most of my family is on the East Coast."

"Do you have a big family?" I asked.

"Two bothers and two sisters."

"That's a pretty big family," I said. "Where are you in the lineup?"

"Right smack dab in the middle," Todd replied.

"What a place to be!"

"Who are you telling?" Todd said in mock surprise as she sipped on his Jack Daniels and Coke.

"What about you?" he ventured. "Tell me about your family."

For some reason I had always hated talking about my family, I guess mainly because my family was a bit, well, different.

"Well, I have a twin sister," I began.

"Really?" he replied, noticeably interested. "Do you two look just alike?"

"No, thank God, we're fraternal twins."

"Ah, I see," he nodded, "but that must be kind of cool, being a twin and all."

"Honestly," I answered, "it probably doesn't feel any different than anything else, since that is all I know." I knew what I meant, but I wasn't sure I was making sense to Todd.

"So it's just you and your sister, then?" he continued.

"No, actually I have an older brother."

"Are you close to your siblings?"

I really had to think about that one. I figured I would have to say no, for reasons that I really couldn't explain. I mean, I do talk to them, but, well, I don't really talk to them.

"Yes, I am." I hated lying to Todd, but I wasn't ready to tell him why I wasn't all that close to my brother or twin sister.

As we continued to talk and I slowly got tipsy on my Chardonnay, I felt a real connection with Todd, something I had not felt in very, very long time. It was definitely a connection that I wanted to explore more.

4 · THE RIDE OF A LIFETIME

TODD AND I HEADED out of Blackbird and waited outside for a cab. The night was still young and neither one of us wanted it to end, so I suggested we head to my place and chill out a bit. I had some wine, and we both had the desire to keep getting to know one another.

I glanced over at Todd as he stared straight ahead, in his own distant place. He was wearing a pair of dark black jeans and a crisp button-up blue top, and the aroma coming from him almost brought tears to my eyes. He smelled so good, or should I say "delicious." I smiled to myself as I wondered what would happen once we got back to my place. I was holding strong to my "new thing," I really was, but I had to be honest, Simone's odds of winning that twenty bucks were looking real good during the cab ride.

We arrived at my building in about 20 minutes, entered the

lobby, and headed for the elevators.

"Penny for your thoughts?" Todd said, breaking the silence as we approached the elevators.

I'd always wondered why people used that saying, as it made no sense at all to me, not to mention my thoughts were worth way more than a penny. But none of that really mattered. No need to break the moment.

"Nothing really," I smiled as I looked down, thankful this man could not read my mind.

"Nothing, huh, so what's up with the big grin?" he asked.

My smile turned into a blush. I felt my face get hot, and was hoping that I wasn't turning red.

"Ah, she blushes, now I'm really intrigued," Todd laughed gently. He leaned back and crossed his arms, waiting for me to spill the beans.

I shifted my weight from left to right, and then back again. Todd made me nervous, but in a good way.

"Okay, if you must know." I bit my bottom lip, feeling a slight sting of pain. I couldn't believe I was about to formulate my private thoughts into words, so I took a deep breath, cleared my throat, and said, "Well, I was just thinking how I have this, this strong desire, to, uh, sleep with you tonight." There. I said it.

"Really?" he asked.

"Yes."

"Hmmm." Todd stroked his goatee as if halfheartedly grooming it.

I looked Todd dead in the eyes. "But I can't."

Todd raised his left eyebrow. "And why is that?"

"Because sleeping with you on the first date would make me look like, well, a ho."

"A ho?

"A ho.

"Really?"

"Yes," I said firmly.

"Hmmm." Todd stroked his goatee again; I guess that was his way of processing his thoughts.

"Does that 'hmmmm' stand for a 'yes' or a 'no'?" I asked, eagerly awaiting his response.

"That would be a 'no'."

"Seriously?" I asked.

"Yes."

"You mean no," I said, correcting him.

"Exactly," Todd replied, a smile crawling across his face.

"Interesting," I said.

"Why so interesting?" he asked.

"Because the average man would think the other."

"This is true," he said, "but I'm not your average man."

"Really?"

"Yep."

"Hmmm. Well, if that's the case," I continued, "let me ask you something."

"Okay."

I took three slow steps toward Todd and leaned in with my lips inches away from his neck. I could smell the intoxicating aroma of his cologne, and it made me melt like an ice cube on a hot summer day.

"So," I whispered, "seeing that you're not the 'average man' then tell me – if I were to kiss you here, would you think I was, you know, a ho?" I gently kissed Todd on his neck, slowly turning it into a seductive lick as I made a circle with my tongue.

Todd looked down at me and smiled. "That would be a 'no.'"

"Hmmmm, okay," I sighed. "Well, what if I did this?" I allowed my tongue to trail up his neck towards his chin and back down again.

Todd let out a sigh as he quickly gathered his composure. "Nope, not at all," he said, eyes narrowing.

I then took my right hand and slowly glided up Todd's

chest. I unbuttoned the two middle buttons, sliding his shirt over to reveal his erect nipple. I looked up at Todd and he looked down at me. Todd licked his lips, then said, "Still 'no.'"

"Well, that's good to know, but what if I took it one step further?" I asked.

"You could do that," Todd said with confidence.

I took Todd's left nipple in my mouth and began sucking it ever so softly. I circled it with my tongue three times before devouring it with my mouth. Todd let out a small moan. I stopped, looked up, and asked, "Well?"

Todd smiled, raising one eyebrow. "Nada, still not a ho to me."

I took a step back, stared directly into Todd's eyes. "So none of the above would makes me a ho, huh?"

"Not in my book." Todd licked his lips like he had something sweet on them. I smiled and I looked down to see the bulge in his pants growing larger. I glided my hand over him, felt it throb. I was wet.

The elevator came, the doors opened and we stepped in. Our stares were intense. I looked at Todd, he looked at me. I leaned back against the wall as I pressed button "22" for my floor. The elevator began to slowly climb.

"So," I challenged him, "if none of that what I did makes me a ho, then what would?"

Todd smiled, stroked his goatee for the third time and then stepped close to me. I felt his manhood hard up against me. "This!" Todd said, grabbing me around my waist and quickly pulling me against him. In seconds we were devouring each other like the starving homeless. Todd's left hand was squeezing and groping my breast as his right hand slid down my stomach to my throbbing love zone only to come back up on the inside of my thigh and under my skirt. Todd pulled off my thong as I quickly unbuckled his Kenneth Cole belt and released the five-O-one button holding it all together. Todd's manhood pushed hard against his zipper, so with one smooth move I unzipped him and release the caged beast.

The elevator continued to go up as I went down, down to pleasure Todd with my hand. I needed to know what I was working with before the main attraction began. I glided Todd out of his jeans and was pleasantly surprised and relieved at the same time. I began to stroke the shaft of his penis as I gently kissed his neck and chest. Todd began to moan as his eyes closed and head fell back against the elevator wall.

I made my way to his face, then our lips connected as we began to kiss deeply. Todd grabbed my arms and quickly pushed me up against the opposite wall as he pulled my right leg up onto his hip, dipped down, and slowly entered his hard throbbing penis into me. I felt a surge of excitement race through my body as Todd reached down and grabbed my left leg, bringing it up to him as he pushed deeper inside of me. We moved in rhythmic sync as I clamped my legs tighter around his waist, so tight that Todd let go of them and braced his hands against the wall in front of him. I grabbed his arms as his thrusts pushed deeper inside me. Our kiss was magnetic, sensual, and erotic. I felt the sweat rolling down my chest and into my belly button. We locked eyes as he took his right hand and put it under my ass, and pushed himself even deeper inside. I let out a loud moan, feeling myself racing to my climax. The elevator was slowly moving up, up, up to the 22nd floor. The anticipation of someone entering the elevator made me even more excited and nervous all at once.

Todd began to kiss my chest, my neck, and my face. "I'm gonna cum," he wheezed, out of breath. "Here I cum!" he repeated, thrusting faster and faster and harder and harder. A warm sensation surged throughout my body.

"Oh, god, oh, god, oh fuuuuuuuuuuuck!"

I climaxed, then Todd. Our bodies went limp as my legs dropped back to the floor, right then left. Todd leaned his heavy body against mine trying to catch his breath as if he had just run a 100-meter dash in nine seconds flat. The elevator finally hit the 22nd floor and the doors opened. Todd looked at me and smiled.

"Thank God for slow elevators," he said.

"Amen to that," I said as we laughed together.

5 · MY BROTHER'S KEEPER

I WAS WATCHING ONE of my favorite movies, *The Thomas Crown Affair*, when I heard a faint knock at the door. It was Sunday evening and I wasn't expecting any company. The faint knock came again as I jumped up from the couch and headed for the door. I opened it to see my older brother, Raymond Edwards.

"Hey sis," Raymond said in his usual sheepish voice.

"Hey."

Raymond was four years older than Mila and me and, well, he looked more like ten. For as long as I could remember my brother had been doing drugs. Started out with an innocent joint here and there while in high school, but now at age 38, he has moved to bigger and more effective ways of getting high – you know, the ones that make you forget to bathe, brush your teeth, and eat. I looked at my brother with his dirty clothes and gaunt face, the picture of an addict. A very handsome man, but it was getting hard to see it under years of chemical abuse and after a lifetime of nights on the streets.

I took a deep breath. I wasn't feeling like company right then, not to mention the fact that, if Raymond was at my doorstep, he needed either a hot meal, a few bucks, or just a warm bed to crash in for a while. I gave him a smile to show that I was happy to see him; he returned one back to me.

"You wanna come in?" I asked as I stepped back to let my brother in. He entered and walked hesitantly over to my terra-cotta leather chaise and sat down. I took my spot on the couch waiting for him to talk, to tell me what was on his mind. Raymond always looked nervous; he was never comfortable around people outside his so-called drug "family." He carried the burden of guilt for allowing this drug to take over his life and isolate him from his family and true friends – although my family, come to think of it, had really isolated him. My mother, father, and twin sister just decided one day that they couldn't help him anymore.

Or maybe they just got tired of trying.

"So, so, what's new, sis?" Raymond stammered, rubbing his hands together as if it were 20 degrees and he was standing in front of a fire barrel trying to stay warm.

"Nothing much, just working on a new campaign."

"Well, you look good, sis. Healthy, I mean," Raymond said, nodding his head. "Picked up some weight too, I see. You always were a little thin, but now you're looking like a woman."

"Thanks," I said, thinking that was a backward compliment if I'd ever heard one, but I'd take it.

"So how are you, Raymond? How are you holding up?"

"Ah, well, not so good sis. Lost my job yesterday."

"You lost your job at the Sox stadium? What happened?" I asked with obvious concern in my voice.

"I came up short, so they thought I was pocketing some of

the money. But I swear I didn't take nothin', they just didn't like me, sis."

I looked at Raymond, wanting to believe him but knowing deep down inside he had taken that money for his habit. Lying becomes a way of life to an addict; it's actually a means of survival on the streets.

"So now I'm, I'm a little short on my rent this month, you know, over at the Charter House. If you're one day late they'll kick you out, no questions asked." Raymond was trying his best to explain his unfortunate situation in a way that would make him out to be the victim and draw sympathy from.

The Charter House was a place over on Roosevelt and Canal Street where drug addicts and homeless people can rent rooms by the week. The place wasn't the cleanest but it was better than sleeping on the streets.

"I don't want to lose my room, sis. It's getting cold outside, ya know?" Raymond said, rocking back and forth on the edge of the chair.

"How much do you need?"

"Not much, not much at all. I think one fifty will get me by. I could even buy some groceries, ya know."

Groceries to a crackhead come in small plastic baggies complete with a glass pipe. And by the look of my brother's 150-pound frame, I guessed he hadn't bought groceries in a long time.

"How about I go over there and pay your rent for you and then I'll take you to the grocery store myself?" I offered, sitting up on the couch.

"I, I, I don't want to put you out, sis. I can handle it myself, ya know. I'm a grown man."

I heard the desperation in my brother's voice and wondered if this was going to be his way of life from now till the end. Seven rehab attempts and a near-death experience hadn't yet shown my brother that there is a better life out there. I know that with an addict you have to let them decide when they want help, and until that happens they will continue to live the life of self-destruction.

"Let me go get my purse."

"Thanks sis, thank you so much," Raymond said as he wiped the snot off his nose with his sleeve.

I walked to my room wondering what had gone wrong, how Mila and I had turned out okay, but our oldest brother hadn't quite made it. I stood in the middle of my room and said a little prayer for him as I picked up my purse, pulled out 150 bucks, and headed back to the living room.

I handed Raymond the money and he quickly stuffed it in the pocket of his dirty, stained jeans.

"Thanks sis, I really appreciate this. I'm gonna pay you back when I get my new job."

"That's fine, Raymond."

I walked Raymond to the door and opened it for him; he took two steps out into the hallway, but quickly turned back around. "How's mom and dad?" My heart sunk upon hearing Raymond say those words; I knew how much it hurt him that they didn't want anything to do with him anymore, I mean, how could they tell their high society friends that they had a son living on the streets, strung out on drugs?

"They're good. I um, I'm actually going to see them next week."

"Good. Well, maybe tell them I said 'hi' and that I've been thinking about them."

"I will."

Raymond looked me deep in my eyes. "One day I'm going to pick myself up, sis," Raymond said as tears formed in his eyes. He quickly wiped them away before they had a chance to dance down his face.

"I know you will Raymond. I know."

He turned and walked down the hallway and into the elevator. Each time he left me, I always wondered if that was the last time I would ever see him alive.

6 · I AM WOMAN, HEAR ME ROAR

MY MOTHER HAD A way of interrogating me. I swear, this woman should have worked for the FBI. She knew how to find your weak spot and go in for the kill.

Don't get me wrong, I love my mother to death, but she can truly drive me crazy with her bourgeois and elitist ways, a trait my twin sister shares with her wholeheartedly, so it is not surprising that they get along so well. I always feel like the third wheel when I am with them, kinda like that Electric Company song, "Which one of these doesn't belong?"

My mother's favorite pastime is entertaining in her home. My favorite pastime? A mind-blowing orgasm and a good book and I will be A-okay. But not my mother; she would not know what to do with herself if she didn't throw a lavish dinner party at least once a month, twice if she really wanted to go all out.

My take on it all? She loves to show off her house and all the expensive things in it. I mean, what's the point of going shopping in Italy, Paris, and Japan if you can't throw it in the faces of your envious friends and family, right?

Growing up in my house was like being on display. I think Mila and I were more like my mother's dress-up dolls than children. She loved to dress us up and take us out. I had my first pair of Prada shoes when I was five – I didn't know what the hell Prada was, but I was sportin' 'em, like a champ. That was probably the beginning of my shoe fetish. Yes, I believe I owe all that to my mother.

It was around six o'clock when I finally got to my parents' house. Although I grew up on the South Side of Chicago in a neighborhood called Hyde Park, after I graduated from high school my parents packed up and headed south, way south, to an upscale suburb called Olympia Fields.

I arrived early with my regular bottle of Dom Perignon for my mom and a box of Cuban cigars for my dad. I was always underdressed. My casual wear never compared to their "after five" attire.

My mother spotted me coming down the hallway. At 57 years old, my mother was a vision of beauty and was often compared to Diahann Carroll.

"Oh, hello darlin'," my mother said as she gave me an air peck on the cheek. She then proceeded to scan me up and down. I was wearing my favorite pair of Via Spiga shoes with a pair of straight leg jeans and a turquoise fitted top, I thought I was looking quite nice, unfortunately my mother though differently. "Look at you. Couldn't you at least put on one thing with sequins?"

"Does underwear count?" I asked, knowing this would rub my mom the wrong way.

"Oh, sweetheart, don't be vulgar," my mother said.

Mother was very conservative. I often wondered if she

and my dad had sex anymore, not to mention if she ever found it in her heart to give him a blowjob.

"Where's Dad?" I asked as I placed the bottle and cigars on the counter, then opened the fridge and grabbed a bottle of Evian.

"You know your father, he's up in his study, and who knows if he'll even show his face tonight."

My father was known as the strong, silent type. He didn't say much, but when he did, it was pretty powerful. I often wondered what he said to get a woman like my mother to even look at him. Then again, as a state Supreme Court justice at age 35, I guess he didn't have to say much at all to hook a woman ten years his junior in search of a "financially stable" life.

I wasn't in the house for five minutes when I hear, "So Mila tells me you met a man." My mother looked at me, waiting for confirmation.

I choked on my water. "Did she? And what else did Mila say?"

"That he is a lawyer and is in the process of opening up his own practice."

I was sure my mother had already "Googled" the brother and knew more about him than I did, but of course she would never admit to being a second-hand stalker.

"Well, it looks like Mila has filled you in pretty well," I said.

"Yes, but when were you going to tell me?"

I shifted a little nervously, preparing to blurt out my lie. "Tonight. I was going to tell you tonight, and he was actually going to come, but he is swamped at work."

"I see," Mother said slowly. "And how long have you been dating him?"

Although in truth it was closer to a month, that wouldn't have flown with my mom since she expected to meet any new love interest within the first week of my making his acquaintance, so out popped Lie Number Two: "Oh, just a little over a week." At least I was consistent with the lies.

"Well, I think that's fabulous," she said. "I'm glad you found a man with a career this time."

"What does that mean?" I retorted. I knew where she was taking this and I hated her for it.

"I mean, if you're going to spend some time with someone, why not have it be a man who can financially support you? Dating men without a real job is just a waste."

"Mom, I don't need a man to support me," I said, "I have a job, a good one."

"Yes, I know, but when you have kids you can't work and raise a decent family."

"Oh, God!" I exclaimed.

"A woman should be at home with her kids. Those first four years are the most important, and you see I didn't work."

"That was your choice," I replied. "I like having a career, my own money, my own say."

That hit home for my mother. She looked away, pretending to straighten the gourmet spice rack. I just couldn't keep my foot out of my mouth.

"I'm sorry, Mom."

As usual, my mom acted like nothing had been said. She was good at brushing such "situations" under the rug. She and Mila definitely had that in common.

"So how is your job going, darlin'?"

I looked at my mom, and felt so sorry for her in that moment. But then I gave into her rules – we just didn't talk about our problems in this house.

"It's um, going great. Simone and I just landed Bianca as a new client."

My mother's face turned up as if she had just sucked on a lemon. "Sweetheart, who is Bianca?"

"She's a singer/songwriter and she's coming out with

her own line of jeans, so Simone and I are working on an intense advertising campaign. It's going to be amazing"

"Well good, good, I'm happy for you. How is Simone anyway, did she get my invite?"

"Yes, mother, she's coming tonight."

"Fabulous. Oh dear, look at the time, I must go change before the guests arrive. Like I said, your father is in his study, and he would love to see you."

My mother turned to leave.

I stood in my parents' obscenely oversized kitchen, with bamboo wood cabinets, stainless steel appliances, and a host of other decorative touches out of some interior design magazine, and thought to myself; Money is great and it's comforting and it will buy you all the pleasures of life – but unfortunately, it will never buy happiness.

•

The night was nearly over when I found an opportunity to pull Simone away from the crowd over to a secluded corner, hoping no one could hear.

"I knew it, it was those damn shoes!" Simone said as I told her every single detail about my elevator escapade with Todd.

Simone held out her hand for her twenty bucks. "So much for the 'waiting to get to know him' thing, so pay up, bitch."

I playfully slapped Simone's hand down.

"I don't know what came over me," I said.

"I do. Dick! It happens to the best of us," Simone said as she grabbed her glass of wine and raised it in a toast. "Now that's something I will definitely drink to. I wish my husband would fuck me in an elevator. Hell, I wish he'd just fuck me period, and maybe then I would stop having thoughts of smothering his ass with a pillow while he slept."

"So do you think Todd'll think I'm a ho?"

"Let's only hope." Simone grinned.

"Come on Simone, be serious," I pleaded.

"I am being very serious. Listen, you fucking this man only means you liked him and you weren't afraid to show it, period. More women should learn from you."

"So you think he'll call me?" I asked, still not totally convinced.

"If he doesn't, then you call him."

"I can't do that," I protested.

"Why not?"

"Because I don't want to look like – "

"A ho?" Simone asked.

"Well, yeah."

"Kai, what is your fixation on looking like a ho? Hell, it's the 21st century; we are in a sexual revolution. Women are finally accepting the fact that it's okay to get our fuck on and if it's with a younger man, even better. Men have been doing it since the beginning of time, so it's our turn, don't you think? So don't be ashamed if you wanna fuck your man on a first date in the elevator. Be ecstatic and call his ass the next day so you can have part two."

Simone downed the rest of her wine. "And if some frigid bitch has something to say, well, fuck her, too." Simone slammed her wine glass down on the table. "Simone has spoken."

"You're crazy, you know that?"

"No, sweetheart. Just horny."

Simone winked and walked away. I looked to the left, then to the right, making sure I was still in the clear.

Simone was 100% right and I knew it; I just needed to hear her validation to convince myself. I couldn't get Todd out of my mind, I knew I had to see him again, for part two, just like Simone said. With that I pulled out my cell phone and dialed his number.

I am woman. Hear me roar!

7 · WHEN IT'S RIGHT, IT'S *SOOO* RIGHT

TODD KNEW EXACTLY WHERE to touch me to make my whole existence quiver. My body was still tingling from our morning lovemaking. This day marked our fourth month together – yep, that's right, Todd had made it through my three-month course and graduated to full-fledged boyfriend, and I couldn't have been happier.

I stretched, fighting sleep as I looked across my bedroom through the slightly opened bathroom door to see the silhouette of my man's beautiful body as he toweled off from his shower. The sun had yet to rise, but that never stopped Mr. Early Riser from starting his day. Todd was a morning person. I unfortunately was not. But I never let this small difference stop me from getting some great loving from him.

I turned and looked at the clock – 5:45am. I lay there staring at the ceiling, noticing some cracks and indentations for the very first time. The fan squeaked as it circulated the scent of our morning lovemaking throughout the room. My naked body felt soft as I glided my hand up and down my toned stomach, then up towards my breast. I played with my nipples. I turned to see Todd watching me; his manhood slowly rising as my self-exploration had triggered his willingness for another go-round.

I winked; he smiled as he walked towards me, growing larger with each step. Todd approached the bed and kneeled down. He slowly glided his hands over my calves. He started to suck each of my toes tenderly and passionately. I moaned, he moaned louder. I closed my eyes as the wetness from his mouth covered each toe then inched up my body. My back slowly arched, almost on cue, as he reached my inner thighs. His hands slowly separated my legs for easy access as he slowly outlined my love nest with his tongue, then headed back down between my thighs. I moaned with excitement and anticipation. Todd then moved back up, this time to explore and taste me before he entered me ever so slowly.

His body was heavy, his manhood firm. We moved in cosmic sync. He pushed deeper inside me but I pulled back, not wanting to cum yet. I wanted to feel the pleasure Todd was giving me a little while longer. He pulled my legs onto his shoulders and went in deeper while he rotated with each thrust.

I tried to talk but my words were no more than low, sensual grunts. Todd kissed my chest, my neck, my lips; he made it a point not to leave any part of my body unexplored, untouched, unloved. I breathed my satisfaction into his mouth; he breathed it back with the same intensity.

Just when I thought it was over, Todd pulled out, flipped me over and entered from behind. I cringed with pleasure.

"Oh, God, baby, you are working me this morning," I groaned.

"And you're lovin' it. Say you love it," Todd demanded.

"You know I do, you know I love it," I agreed passionately.

Todd began to thrust faster and faster and faster. He slapped my ass; it stung with immense pleasure and the second slap felt even better. With the third slap he pulled out and in seconds we were back face-to-face. We stared into each other's eyes as we communicated our love without words. I felt the sweat drip down my back as my climax approached rapidly.

"Baby, baby, I'm about to cum," I said.

Todd buried his face in my neck as he thrust harder and harder, faster and faster as he approached his orgasm in zero point five seconds.

"I'm about to cum," he shouted.

"Me, me, me tooooooooooooooooooooooo!"

We climaxed together, Todd's body collapsing on mine. Our sweat mixed together into one large love spot, right on my 700- thread count sheets.

•

I woke to the sound of the shower. The sun was sneaking through the manufactured holes of my navy blue curtains, leaving a striped pattern on the honey-apple hardwood floor. I turned to see the clock, which displayed 7am. I took a deep breath as I began to plan my day in my head.

The shower turned off and Todd opened the door, steam escaping as if running for freedom. He began to lotion his body, calves, thighs, stomach, back and face.

My mouth was dry. I reached for the half-full bottle of water that lay near my nightstand. I drank the rest and laid it back down. I looked up to see Todd in all his nakedness. He stared at me, then at the bottle. He smiled; I smiled back.

"You're just going to leave that right there, aren't you?"

I looked back down to see the water bottle on the floor. "Nope, I'm going to throw it away," I said.

"Uh-huh," Todd replied, "just like the others."

My eyes glided over the floor. Three more water bottles.

"Well, at least they're in a neat row," I said with a childish grin.

Todd shook his head as he walked towards me; his body was muscular and cut to perfection. Todd had the type of body that didn't need the gym 24/7; he was naturally fit and I loved every inch of it.

Todd sat on the edge of the bed as he opened the drawer and took out his underwear and a pair of black socks.

"So what do you have planned for today?" I asked as I rubbed his smooth, baby-soft back.

"My contractor is coming over to inspect my office, remember?" he said. "I need to add a conference room upstairs."

I stretched and yawned. "Oh, right," I said.

For eight months Todd had been working toward getting his own practice. And his dream was about to become a reality. The one thing that I loved about Todd, is when he put his mind to something, he didn't stop until his goal was reached. From time to time he would add me to his list of accomplishments, but quiet as I kept, I was determined to make him mine the moment I laid eyes on him. But I'd let him think he wore me down.

"What are you doing for lunch today?" Todd asked me as he slid on his faded paper-cloth jeans.

"Simone and I have a meeting with a potential new client. We're trying to add two more to our roster. Why, what's up?"

"Alana wants to have lunch and I want you to meet her."

I sat up upon hearing the name of another woman.

"Who?"

"Alana, my old roommate from college."

"The model?" I asked, knowing the answer but needing confirmation.

"Well, not anymore, since she had her daughter, but she's working at getting back into it, I'm sure."

Todd turned and grabbed a white t-shirt from the second drawer – his designated drawer at my house. I have the third and fifth drawer in his dresser as well as a section in his closet.

What can I say? I love to shop.

"So you're having lunch with her?" I asked.

"Yes, baby, and I want you to come with," Todd said as he grabbed a bigger t-shirt and pulled it over the white one.

"Well, I can't, sweetie," I said, trying to keep the tinge of jealousy out of my voice. "I told you I have a meeting. Why can't I meet her another day?"

"Because she's only going to be in Chicago for a few days."

"Okay, well, when is she coming back?" I asked, not really caring but trying to keep the conversation flowing.

"She'll be back for the opening of my practice, so I guess you guys can meet then," Todd said as he gave me a look.

"That's next month?" I stated as a question, although I knew the exact date and location.

"Don't act like you don't remember," Todd said.

Todd sat back down on the bed and looked me dead in my sleepy eyes.

"Baby, Alana is my best friend, nothing more, okay? Besides, she is looking forward to meeting you."

"Is that so? Well then, I am looking forward to meeting her, too."

"No, you're not, but it's okay," said Todd. "Once you meet her you'll love her."

"Love is a strong word," I replied.

Todd kissed me softly on the lips. "That it is, so be careful how you throw it around." He winked, then stood and said, "I gotta run, so I'll call you later. If you change your mind, we're meeting at Butter at 1pm."

"Where is that again?"

"It's on South Green between Adam and Monroe."

"Got it," I said as I sat up, preparing to make my transition to the shower.

"Bye, baby," Todd blew me a kiss and headed out the door.

I lay back down, staring at the ceiling once again. I wondered if those cracks were there when I moved in this place. I wondered if Alana was as pretty as I feared.

8 · INQUIRING MINDS WANT TO KNOW

OUR ADVERTISING CAMPAIGN WAS coming along wonderfully. Simone and I were steadily putting together a series of commercials, print ads, and billboards.

Simone's office was filled with every single type of jean and t-shirt that "Bianca" was coming out with. We knew this was going to be our ticket to the top, so we were putting our blood, sweat and tears into it.

I entered Simone's office as she sat staring at an ad board.

"Hey, you," I said, closing the door behind me.

"Hey, yourself," Simone said, not even looking up.

"What's going on?" I inquired as I walked over to see what Simone was staring at so intently.

"Our print ads are going up in less than two months and I'm not loving this model."

I walk around to Simone's side of the desk, to give it another look, this time from the perspective from which Simone was no longer "loving" the model for the campaign.

"Yeah, I can see that. She doesn't really do anything for the clothes."

"Or the campaign, for that matter."

Simone picked up her phone. "Amanda," she said, "contact the Ford agency and get them to send over ten Zed cards of new models for our "Bianca" campaign.

Simone hung up.

"You're serious about replacing her, huh?" I half-asked as I made my way back around Simone's desk and had a seat across from her.

"Hell, yeah, we've spent too much time on this to have it ruined by a shapeless, no-spark model."

I loved Simone's attitude; when she was over something, she was so over it, not to mention that she had no problem making a decision on the spot. While some are quick to waver back and forth, Simone sets her mind on something and it's done.

"You hungry?" she asked. "I'm going to order in some Sushi for lunch."

"Yeah, that sounds good." I watched Simone as she ordered our lunch. I needed to talk, and although I hated bringing my personal life into the office, my concentration was suffering and I needed my girls ear and input.

Simone was off the phone so I seized the moment before she could get off on another tangent.

"Can I ask you a question?" I asked as I uncrossed my left leg and crossed it over my right.

"Sure," Simone answered.

"It's not business-related. Do you mind?"

"Girl, please, of course not! What is it?" Simone asked as she looked up from her MacBook.

"How would you feel if your man's best friend was a woman?"

"Hmm, I don't know," she said. "Why?"

"Would you feel intimidated?"

Simone looked up at me and closed the cover on her laptop. "Where is this going?"

"Okay," I said. "Todd's best friend is here."

"And let me guess – she's a woman," Simone said.

"Yep."

Simone pondered the question for a minute. "Depends on how she looks," Simone said as she sipped on her Evian water. I could tell her mind was turning.

She put down her Evian, sat back and folded her arms. "Now if she looks like she escaped from Lincoln Park Zoo," Simone began, "I wouldn't worry about it, men very rarely are friends with ugly women – unless, of course, they're trying to get to the prettier, sexier girlfriend, then they'll be her best pal ever. Now if she has a halfway decent face with a great body, then hell yeah. Especially if the body is all that. See, men will forgo an average face for a fuckable body in a second."

I knew Simone would have a great answer because she's not only perceptive, she knows how to get straight to the point and that was exactly what I needed.

"I say all that," Simone continued, "to bring me to my main point."

Simone leaned in as if she was about to say something so profound that she wanted to make sure I didn't miss a syllable.

"Whenever there are two organs of the opposite sex involved in a so-called 'friendship' they will eventually collide, over and over again," she said. "And the next thing you know your man is fucking his female friend. I mean, let's be real, we are human."

"So what should I do?" I asked her. "I mean, Todd swears nothing is going on between him and Alana."

"Do you believe him?" Simone asked, raising one suspicious eyebrow.

"Yeah, I guess," I said. "He really hasn't given me any reason not to. Not to mention, they have been friends since they were thirteen. In all honesty, if they were going to do something don't you think they would have by now?"

Simone leaned back up and tilted her head to the right. "What makes you think they haven't?"

Simone had one valid point.

I sat straight up in my seat. "You think?"

Simone sat back.

"Anything is possible. If you like I could always trip the bitch down a flight of stairs. No one likes fucking a paraplegic."

Simone made me spit my water out, right there on the table. She would come out of the box with crazy comments like that from time to time that invariably made me lose all composure.

"My suggestion? Wait until you meet her, sniff her out, see how they interact. I wouldn't get all upset over something you haven't even sized up yet. Hell, she could be Magilla's cousin for all we know."

"This is true, you're right," I said as I relaxed back into my seat.

"Of course I'm right, mama's always right, and don't you forget that."

Simone gave me a wink. I let out a sigh of momentary relief.

Even though I'm sure she was not in the Magilla family, for some odd reason I felt a little bit better.

9 · TO EACH HER OWN

IF BEAUTY HAD A name, it would be Alana Brooks.

The moment Alana walked into Todd's newly renovated office space, I knew it was her, the best friend Todd had been talking about since we first met. The best friend that he's known since he was thirteen, the best friend that he took to the Senior Prom, the best friend that was his college roommate, the best friend that he could sleep in the same bed with and nothing would ever go down – the best friend that was not only a former Essence print model, but my man's best friend. Fuck!

I think the room stopped just to watch Alana walk. I had no idea she would look this way; I pictured a Vivica Fox on a bad day, but no, Alana was five eleven and perfect. Her hair was short and cut ever so perfect to her face, her eyes were big and alive and she had a way of smiling that would light up any dark place.

I watched as Alana walked my way, with runway residue in each step. I instantly felt self-conscious. I couldn't help my mind from racing through all of the other wardrobe options I could have chosen for myself on this occasion to make me look way sexier. I felt a sense of immediate competition. I wanted to freeze time, just long enough to run my ass upstairs and change into my "I can be sexy, too" dress with matching attitude. But unfortunately the powers to be had other plans for me. Yep, you guessed it: total humiliation with a nice big helping of fading self-esteem.

I watched as Todd's eyes light up like that stupid New Year's Eve ball in Times Square and jealously wondered if that was how he looks at me when I catwalk across a room? My first urge was to hate Alana, but her only crime was her ability to turn more heads than me, and well, that just wasn't enough.

Or was it?

I glanced across the room to catch Simone checking Alana out as well. Simone shot me a look and made a joking gestured as if tripping someone down a flight of stairs. I couldn't help but chuckle. I needed to laugh right about then because what was happening just wasn't funny. Alana finally made it over to where Todd and I were standing.

"Todd Anthony!" Alana announced his first and middle name with enough energy to fuel a Boeing 747, and then proceeded to give my man a full bear hug.

"Hey, you made it!" Todd exclaimed, grinning from ear to ear.

"Are you kidding me? Miss your grand opening? Never!"

"Alana, this is my girlfriend Kai, Kai, this is Alana."

"Nice to meet you," we said in unison. I made a silent wish then, but I knew that it didn't come true, because Alana was still standing in front of me.

Todd, you didn't say Kai was so beautiful." Alana said as she shot me a big smile.

"Well you know how I do." Todd said with too much confidence.

"Thank you, Alana, that's sweet of you to say." I said, mirroring her smile.

That compliment took me off guard, but I'll take it!

"So where is Avery?" Todd asked Alana as he grabbed a few hors d'oeuvres off the passing tray.

"He's in training camp down in Texas. He'll be there for the next four weeks."

Alana was married to the number one running back in the NFL, Avery Anderson, and although they looked like the picture perfect couple, she was not happy. At least according to Todd. Apparently her athlete husband does a better job of cheating on her in scoring with the groupies, as opposed to scoring touchdowns, which he was actually getting paid to do.

I guess it really doesn't matter how beautiful you are, if a man wants to cheat, he will cheat. For the professional athletes, particular the NBA and NFL, pussy may of well be served up on a silver platter.

I began to feel a bit out of place as Alana and Todd started reminiscing about their college days at Howard. I was seconds from walking away, when Alana touched my arm.

"So Kai, I hear you're in advertising."

The sound of Alana's voice directed towards me threw me off. I had been slowly detaching, but Alana quickly pulled me back in.

"I am. I work for McKenzie and Strong over on Michigan Avenue."

"I did some work for them years ago, pre-baby, I mean. Now this whole midsection is just not camera-ready."

"How old is your baby?" I asked.

"She's 15 months," Alana said as she shot Todd a look, "and Todd is the godfather." Alana started rubbing Todd's arm.

I watched as Alana rubbed Todd's arm a bit too long for my liking. But I had to keep reminding myself that they are just friends, they are just friends.

"Well, isn't that sweet, and by the way, you look great after just having a baby," I said.

"You're sweet. But I just hired a trainer and I will be back in the gym this month," she said. "I actually joined Lake Shore Athletic."

"Oh, I didn't know they had a Lake Shore Athletic in New York." I said.

"They don't," said Alana. "I joined the one here in Chicago."

"Really, here in Chicago? Are you planning on staying for awhile?"

"I'm moving here," Alana said.

My heart dropped. Those three words came in super slow speed. A flash of anger shot through my body.

"Didn't Todd tell you?" Alana asked.

"No, actually, Todd did not," I said as I turned to shoot daggers into his neck. Todd shifted uncomfortably. He knew he was in trouble. Big fucking trouble.

"So when is this happening, Alana?"

"In the next month or so," she replied. "Avery just got traded to the Chicago Bears," Alana added with a smile.

"That's great," I said, "but excuse me, I'm going to get more wine."

I headed in the direction of the small office kitchen, hoping Simone saw the rage in my steps. Like a best friend, she did, and she met me in the kitchen.

"Okay, I don't know exactly what was said," Simone said, "but I think I saw smoke coming out of your ears."

"She's moving to Chicago."

"Alana?"

"You got it," I said as I began pacing back and forth in the kitchen.

"You're kidding me!" Simone exclaimed.

"No, and that bastard Todd didn't even mention it to me and I'm sure he's known about it for a while."

"Of course he has," Simone said. "Men have selective memories when it comes to informing us of vital information, especially when it comes to other women."

Just then Todd entered the kitchen.

"Hey Kai," he said. "You okay?"

"What the hell do you think, Todd?" Simone belted out.

"I was asking Kai," Todd shot back.

"Yeah, well, I was answering for Kai," Simone replied indignantly.

"Simone, it's cool," I said quickly, before their exchange started getting out of hand.

Simone gave me a look just to double check. "Fine, I'll be in the living room if you need me."

Simone left the kitchen as I walked over to the refrigerator and pulled out a few bottles of wine.

"So, when were you going to tell me Alana was moving to Chicago?"

Todd took a deep breath as he shifted his weight to his heels and pushed his hands in his pockets . He looked down at the floor then back up at me.

"Baby, it's not a big deal, really."

"Well, if it's not such a big deal then why didn't you tell me?"

"It must've slipped my mind," he said.

"Yeah, right."

"Why are you making such a big deal?" Todd asked. "I mean, you act like I'm fucking her."

"Are you?"

Todd paused, then continued slowly. "No, I'm not. How many times do I have to tell you? We are just friends."

I took a deep breath. I was not nearly drunk enough to deal with that shit. I gathered a few bottles of wine to take into the other room; I needed to get away from this man before I totally snapped. I turned to leave when Todd grabbed my arm, took the bottles from me and put them on the counter.

"Listen Kai," he said, "you are who I want to be with, not Alana. I love you, not her. You have to believe me."

Hearing those words from Todd made me feel a little better, made the jealousy fade a bit.

"I love you too, baby, I just, I just don't like being in the dark," I said. What I really wanted to say, of course, was that I just didn't like beautiful best friends moving to the same city as my boyfriend.

Todd put his arms around my waist.

"I'm sorry," he said. "I promise to keep you abreast of all situations, OK?"

"Abreast?" I said with a chuckle.

"Abreast," Todd repeated, and we shared a well-needed laugh.

"Okay, then," I said as I leaned in and planted an "I am the only woman you need" kiss on him as I reached down to massage his manhood.

"Damn baby, not now, we got guests," Todd said.

"So?" I replied, with a seductive smile.

I was headed in for another kiss when Alana walked in.

"Oh, I see you two are busy," Alana said.

Todd pulled back from me, almost too fast for my liking.

"Hey, no, it's cool," Todd said. "You need anything, more wine?"

"Red wine would be nice," Alana said as she smiled at me. It took everything I had to return the smile. I'm sure it looked a little fake. We held the stare for a moment, then I turned away.

Todd scrambled to fill a glass for Alana and serve it to her.

I glanced back over towards Alana, almost paralyzed at how beautiful this woman was. I replayed in my mind, over and over, what Todd had said to me a few minutes earlier, like a mantra to keep me sane in that moment. It was more than a bit awkward with the three of us sharing that small space.

"Listen," I said, "I'm going to find Simone, because if I don't watch her she could be fondling the help in the bathroom." I chuckled at my own comment – alone.

"Okay, baby," Todd said, planting a kiss on my lips.. "I'll see you in a minute."

I started toward the kitchen door, but turned back to see Todd and Alana enjoying each other's company. I paused to swallow my jealousy before going to look for my best friend, Simone.

10 · A TUG OF WAR

ALANA HAD ONLY BEEN in Chicago for six weeks but I was
already two seconds from slappin' a FedEx label on her ass and
overnighting her back to her home town in Nebraska. Now I
understood that she was Todd's best friend, but since her return
I hadn't seen much of Todd. Well, let me clarify, I hadn't seen
much of Todd without Alana being there, too. She had a way of
making herself available – always. Weekend dinners, walks in
the park, a friendly game of pool or just hanging out at the
house; you name it, Alana was there, as if she had become a
permanent fixture in our relationship. My relationship with
Todd was morphing from a healthy couple to the three muske-
teers.

I was about to snap.

I knew that her famous husband was too busy with his
NFL career (chasing pussy across the U. S. of A.") to give Alana

the attention she needed and desired, but hello, that was neither my concern nor my problem. I didn't sign up to share my man with anyone, especially Alana.

I leaned back as I swiveled around two times in my burgundy-brown leather chair. Work was slow and I was glad; I needed to focus at least 90 percent of my attention on the situation at hand. Translation: I needed to do something fast.

I dialed Todd's work number and, of course, got his overly friendly, overly irritating assistant who told me that he was with a client. I quickly hung up and dialed his cell number, knowing he would not answer. I decided to leave a sexy (but classy) message on his voicemail, letting him know that he had a date that evening with his girlfriend, who wasn't taking "No" for an answer. I then let him know to expect the works that night, no holds barred. I was getting excited just thinking about what I was going to do to him. Todd loved when I left seductive messages on his voicemail and, to be honest, I loved doing it. I considered it foreplay – or should I say pre-foreplay.

I finished up early at work and headed to the ladies' room to touch up my make-up, fluff my hair and spray on his favorite perfume. I was ready to show Todd a night he would remember for, well, at least a month. I took one last glance at myself in the mirror and yes, I was ready to take his ass to the mat, in a good way. Look out WWF, 'cause here comes KWE, better known as Kai – with an "i"!

•

I decided to make reservations at Blackbird, the scene of our first official date. I was a little excited since Todd and I had not had a so-called date in a while. He confirmed that he would be there right after work. I fluffed my hair one last time and checked my make-up; this was going to be a night like the good old days. Todd and I had been living together for about a month; I gave up my cute, adorable and single pad up north and moved in with him downtown near Dearborn Station. I had to admit, living downtown wasn't as bad as I'd thought it would be, and Todd was an added perk. But since our recent transition to cohabitation we had become a bit routine at times, so there was no better time than right then to start spicing things up.

And I knew just how to do it.

I glanced at my watch when I arrived at Blackbird; it was 7:15pm. The Hostess came over to seat me. I thought about waiting for Todd to arrive, but then I figured I might as well head to our table – I could order an appetizer and a few drinks just in time for Todd to arrive.

The Hostess was young and had a fresh, young, innocent appeal. She wore a fashionably tailored white top and form fitted skirt, very simple yet elegant. Her skin was flawless and her makeup was done as if she were going to a photo shoot after her shift. I couldn't help but stare, especially since Simone and I were in search of a new model for our upcoming campaign – and her look would be perfect. She seated me at a corner table, nice and secluded. I figured it would be perfect; in case I wanted to give Todd a foot massage under the table, no one would have to know.

"Have a great dinner," the hostess said as a smile crawled across her butterscotch face.

"Thank you, I will," I said.

The young girl turned to walk away when I added, "Excuse me?"

The young girl turned back around. "Did you need something else?" she asked.

"No, I mean, yes – I was just wondering if you were a model?"

The young girl blushed, looked down, then back up. "No, I'm not, I'm actually a film student at Loyola, why?"

"I was looking for someone to do some print work for me," I replied. "I'm in advertising."

"Oh, that's cool," the girl said. "Well, I did do some modeling in high school, but my passion is to become a director."

"A director, huh?" I wanted to tell her that she could make a ton of money on that face of hers, but who was I to deter her from her dream? "Well good luck with that," I said.

"Thank you, and enjoy your evening," the young girl said, smiled politely and walked away.

I glanced at my watch; it was now 7:30pm, and Todd was officially thirty minutes late. I grabbed my cell phone, dialed his office and heard the machine come on. I then dialed his cell, thinking that maybe he was stuck in traffic, but it went straight to voicemail. Hmmm, why was his cell phone off? I wondered. I then texted him on his cell phone and waited patiently for a response.

7:45pm and still no response. I started to get worried. By eight o'clock my appetite for food, as well as for sex, had been replaced by a slowly growing rage. I paid for my two drinks and one cold appetizer and headed for the front door. The hostess gave me a quizzical look as I politely smiled back and headed out the door. No need to stop and explain why I was leaving – and besides, I needed to find out what happened to Todd.

I hailed a cab and headed home, thinking maybe he forgot about our date. Between Alana and opening his practice he had been very forgetful, especially about things that mattered to me. His drive and focus that were once very attractive to me were now thorns in my side.

I took a deep breath and thought, okay, maybe he is working so hard he lost track of time. I mean, what else could have caused him to stand me up, right?

Wrong. As my cab headed down Randolph towards home, it stopped at a red light and as I turned to my left I saw the unthinkable, the unimaginable, the ultimate fucking no-no – my man and Alana having dinner. Together. That's right, I said to-ge-ther. I couldn't believe what I was seeing. I was hoping it was mistaken identity, but as I stared even harder, I realized it was them.

I told the driver to stop, immediately, as I nearly jumped

out of the cab with it still moving. I walked much purpose toward the restaurant called "Nine" as I focused in on them like a sniper on his prey. I felt heat escaping from my ears, nose, and neck with each step that I took. I picked up my phone and dialed Todd's cell number one last time, but it went straight to voicemail again.

Did this man think I was a fool? What does he think he is going to tell me about how he stood me up on our date to be with Alana, a friend, or so he claims? I felt my heart pumping faster and faster. I approached the door and entered the restaurant, but when the hostess asked me if I had a reservation, I told her I didn't need one and wouldn't be there long. I turned, took a deep breath, and told myself not to make a scene. I was headed their way when Todd looked up to see me marching his way – well, their way. I was going in for a slam-dunk. Todd immediately jumped up to intercept my play.

"What are you doing here?" he said, guiding me back toward the entrance of the restaurant. I jerked away from him.

"What am I doing here? What the hell are you doing here? We had a date tonight."

"Oh shit!" he exclaimed.

Oh shit! Oh shit! Is that all this mofo had to say for standing me up?

"Did you just say 'Oh shit?'" I asked.

"Baby, I can explain," Todd said.

"Please do," I said, "because I cannot wait to hear this one."

"Alana called me at work all upset because she found out that Avery was cheating on her."

"What?"

"Yeah, it's been going on for two years," Todd said. "Crazy, huh?"

"Who gives a shit, Todd? Is that why you stood me up?"

"Kai," he said slowly, "this is serious."

"Serious?" I repeated. "Newsflash, Todd – Avery's an NFL

player, cheating to him is like breathing. Alana knew that when she married him. Hell it's probably written in their fucking vows." My voice was starting to escalate.

"How about you show some sympathy?" he said.

"How about you show some respect?" I shot back sharply.

"Can we talk about this at home?" Todd pleaded. "I will explain everything then, but right now she's really going through it."

"Yeah?" I replied sarcastically. "Tell her to join the fucking club."

"You need to lower your voice," Todd demanded.

"And you need to act like you have a goddamn girlfriend." With that I turned to leave – I didn't really want to, but I did.

"Kai!" he yelled.

"Go to hell!" I yelled back.

By its end, the whole restaurant was tuned in to our little fight, with Alana in the front row.

I headed out to the street to hail a cab. I couldn't believe that Todd wasn't coming after me; he just stood there and let me walk out of the restaurant. Fucking bastard.

For the first time in my life I was hyperventilating. I always thought it was an act when people would do it, but now I knew it could happen because right then I needed a brown paper bag worse than a homeless man needed a bath. I walked down Randolph Street, and could barely feel my feet and legs propelling me forward. I didn't know what to do. I felt helpless, frustrated, angry, and sad. Alana Brooks had a hold over my man that I couldn't seem to penetrate.

•

A few hours later, I was in the bed in a fetal position, trying to hold back the tears, but they had a way of forcing themselves out. I didn't know what to do; I loved Todd with all my heart, and we had an amazing relationship, with just one exception – Alana. Her mere presence was driving a wedge between us and I didn't know what to do.

I heard the front door open and close, so I wiped the tears away and pretended to be asleep. I listened as Todd slowly headed towards the bedroom. The door slowly opened and I could hear him walking towards the bed. I didn't want him near me, but at the same time I longed to be held in his arms. I listened as he took off his shoes, slacks, and shirt. He slowly, carefully slid into bed next to me.

I didn't want to let him know that I was still awake, wondering, worrying, and crying. Todd slid closer towards me and I felt the heat from his body, smelled his cologne, and wanted to cry – but didn't. His hand gently touched my side as he slid his arm around me and a tear fell from my eye. He pulled me into him as I felt his breath on my neck. A lump was quickly forming in my throat as a stream of tears continued down my face. I sniffed; he spoke, in a faint, gentle whisper.

"Baby, please don't be mad. I never intended on standing you up tonight, and I'm sorry. I know it's hard to take that my best friend is a woman, but understand that nothing is going on between us. I love you and only you."

I was silent; the lump in my throat as well as in my heart wouldn't let me speak.

"I wanna make this work. The truth is –" Todd paused to take a deep breath. "Alana was so upset she was contemplating suicide, and I couldn't let her be alone, not at that moment. Sacrificing our night out to be with her was a hard decision to make and I'm sorry, but I promise I will make it up to you."

I listened but did not respond.

Todd nestled his face in my neck, as he kissed it two times. "Baby, I don't want to lose you. I love you."

More tears fell, and my pillow was soaking wet. I couldn't turn to face Todd, not knowing what type of reaction I would have. So I lay there and silently cried. I don't remember when I finally fell asleep, although I do remember Todd's arms around my waist – and a void in my heart.

11 · LIVING IN EMERALD CITY

THE NEXT FEW DAYS were hard to deal with. I felt so confused, I couldn't think straight. Was I being insecure and irrational? Was Todd telling the truth? Was Alana just a friend, or was she positioning herself, waiting for me to walk out the picture? My thoughts bounced back and forth like a ping-pong match; I hate him, I love him, I'm going to dump him, I need to stay with him. The one thing I hated, even despised, was coming off as the insecure girlfriend. That's why I had been biting my tongue all the time.

Dumping Todd would be the ultimate insecure move, not to mention it risked throwing him into Alana's arms, and I can't go out like that. I needed to regroup and figure out how to handle the situation like the creative and intelligent person that I am. I needed a plan, a solution.

I needed Simone.

I dialed Simone's extension and her voicemail came on. I told her that it was imperative that she call me, that I needed to talk about something very important. I hung up and a scant few seconds later my phone rang. Thinking it was Simone calling me back, I was shocked when I heard my assistant telling me I had a visitor. I quickly checked my daily planner, hoping I didn't forget about a meeting or appointment, but I had nothing scheduled. I asked my assistant who my visitor was and she replied, "Alana."

"Shit!" was my initial reaction.

I paused, not knowing what to say next. Why in the hell was she at my job? I mean, hell, Todd's wasn't there, so why was she? I told my assistant to wait five minutes and send her in.

In those five minutes I tried to think of every reason why Alana wanted to talk to me. Was she finally going to tell me that she is in love with my man? Or worse, that my man is in love with her? Or even worse, that they are in love with each other? Shit. I started to feel droplets of sweat forming under my armpits. I didn't like being in situations like this; I hated surprises, especially when they had to do with me.

My assistant buzzed me again. I felt rushed, almost irritated, as I told her to send Alana in.

Alana entered my office, almost apologetic in a way. I could tell by her body language that she was just as nervous as I was, which oddly enough made me feel a little more at ease. I couldn't imagine for the life of me what she wanted, but I knew it had something to do with Todd. We locked eyes as she made her way towards my desk. She wore a mint green wrap dress that hugged her body perfectly. Her hair was slicked back into a small ponytail and her make-up was perfect. I couldn't help but think that whatever this woman puts on, she looks flawless in it. It wasn't fair, and it was almost as if the universe was playing an ongoing joke on me.

"Hey, Kai, I don't mean to bother you, but I really needed

to talk to you," Alana said as she sat down in front of me, crossing her legs and folding her hands in her lap.

"Sure, what's on your mind?" I responded with a convincingly calm demeanor.

Alana began rubbing her hands up and down her skirt as if she were attempting to smooth out the wrinkles, but there was not a single wrinkle to be seen. Alana was nervous.

"About last night, I wanted to apologize for what happened. I was a basket case and well, I didn't know who else to call."

"Actually, it was not a big deal," I said as I swallowed extra hard, knowing damn well it was a huge deal. I hated that I had just said that.

"The way you ran out of the restaurant, I thought, well…" she said, her voice trailing off without finishing.

Alana's hands stopped moving for a second, and then started up again.

"I just thought you were pretty pissed," Alana continued.

I knew that was my chance to correct what I had just said, to tell Alana that I was so freakin' mad I could have body slammed both of them right there in the restaurant. But then I would come off as insecure and jealous – you know, the kind we all read about in those "Dear Abby" columns. I wasn't going out like that. So I took a deep breath and threw on an "I'm cool with it" smile.

"Actually, Alana, I was more disappointed than pissed. I was looking forward to spending last night with my man."

"Believe me, Kai, I understand and I am sorry that I took your night away." Alana shifted in her seat, looked me dead in the eye, and added, "Did Todd tell you what happened with my husband?"

I sat there for a minute wondering if I should tell her that I knew about her cheating husband even before she did.

"Actually he didn't," I lied.

"Well, I don't want to bore you with the details, but long

story short, I'm getting a divorce," she said. "I got married for all the wrong reasons and, well, it's just not working out."

"I'm sorry to hear that," I said with my sincerest voice ever. Of course, I wanted to add, "I guess when you take a vow to love, honor, and fuck everything breathing, things tend to take a turn for the worse." But I didn't.

"Yeah, it's for the best," Alana said.

"I guess everything happens for a reason," I said as we held an awkward stare. In that moment I knew that Alana's divorce translated into sucking even more time away from Todd and me. Could I honestly say she was doing it on purpose? My insecurities said, "Hell fucking yeah!" but my rational side saw a woman who was lonely and needed friends. Either way, something had to change. I needed a plan, and fast.

12 · THE PLAN

"SO WHAT AM I going to do?" I asked Simone as I sat across from her in her office. I couldn't believe that this situation had come down to this, me asking my best friend how to keep Todd's best friend away from him.

Simone sat, contemplating. She took a deep breath, then announced, "This is perfect."

"What?" I said.

"Simply perfect," Simone said again.

"Perfect how?" I was having a hard time seeing exactly what Simone was seeing, but I waited patiently for her explanation.

"Alana's getting a divorce because her husband cheated on her, right?"

"Like a champ," I said.

"Kai, don't you see how perfect this is?" Simone said

again.

"No."

"Honey, when a woman gets divorced there is already a self-esteem factor involved, and it only doubles when the reason she's getting divorced is because her loving husband cheated on her."

I was starting to see where Simone was going with her simply perfect idea.

"Ah, so her self-esteem is probably low right now," I said.

"I'm talking rock fucking bottom, can't get any lower than that," Simone said as her mind continued to churn. "So this is what I propose: we need a new model so we hire her."

"Hire who?"

"Alana."

"What?" I exclaimed. "You can't be serious. I'm not hiring Alana."

"Hear me out, please. We hire Alana and her deflated self-esteem, pump her up, make her feel beautiful again, you know, tell her what she needs to hear right now to lift the suicide bitch up, and at the same time you have a bird's eye view of her, as well as keeping her so busy on our campaign that she won't have time to fart."

"Damn, that is good," I said.

"No, it's fucking brilliant," Simone boasted.

"But is it smart to have her around so much?" I asked.

"Kai, are you familiar with the saying, 'Keep your friends close but your enemies closer'?"

At that moment I got exactly what Simone was trying to do and I loved her even more for it.

"I love you."

"I know," Simone shot back with confidence.

"Now all you have to do is fire that mousy face model I just hired, meet with Alana, and offer her the modeling gig."

"Do you think she'll take it?"

"Please! Can a gay man work a runway?" Simone said,

raising the rhetorical question with a lift of her left eyebrow. She grabbed her daily planner and headed out of her office.

•

I called Alana the next day and asked if she could meet me at Avenue M at noon, a restaurant on North Milwaukee Ave. I clearly let Alana know that I had some very important business to discuss with her. She called me back to say she had to make it 1pm since her nanny wasn't available until 12:30.

Alana arrived 12:45, wearing a white strappy dress that stopped right above her knee and her shoes of choice, a pair of turquoise Prada sandals with a matching purse. Her hair was slicked back into a neat bun and her face looked as if the sun had kissed it. Just a mere glance at Alana made me think that what I was doing was right.

Alana glanced around the restaurant until our eyes connected. I waved, and she smiled as she headed over my way.

"How are you?" I said with surprising enthusiasm. For the first time I was actually happy to see her. She mirrored my enthusiasm.

"Hey, Kai, wow, I was so surprised to get your call. What's up?"

Alana sat down in front of me with eager eyes, and for a split second I started to have second thoughts about going through with Simone's plan – until Alana spoke up.

"I just got off the phone with Todd, and he says 'Hello.'"

The second thoughts quickly vanished so I got right to the point.

"What's up is that Simone and I want to hire you."

Alana had just picked up her glass of water with two lemon wedges in it and damn near choked upon hearing those words.

"Get out! Are you serious?"

"Yeah, we actually need a model for our new campaign and we thought your look would be perfect."

"Wow, you're kidding me!" Alana said as she began to

smooth out her hair and adjust her top. "This is amazing."

"So are you interested?" I asked as I leaned back waiting for her to jump at the offer.

"How much does it pay?" Alana shot back.

"Well, actually, I would have to check with Simone about that," I said slowly, not even expecting that.

I couldn't believe what I was hearing. I wanted to say, "Does it matter how much it pays? You don't have a job and you should be feeling pretty low right now since your husband just cheated on you for the 10th time – this month." But I took the high road.

"Okay, well, check with Simone and let me know," Alana said.

"Okay, I um, I will," I said, a bit irritated and very much taken aback.

"Girl, I'm just messing with you," Alana laughed. "Of course I want the gig, and for the record, I would work for free."

"Really?" I asked. Not that she needed the money.

"Of course not, but I just had to throw that in there to sound enthusiastic," Alana continued in her overly excited voice.

"Of course," I agreed.

Alana pulled out a little mirror and began to primp. "This is so great. I was just telling Todd I wanted to get back into modeling and then bam, you offer me a gig that I didn't even have to audition for. How great is that?"

"Pretty damn great," I said without a trace of sarcasm, shocking even myself.

"So when do I start?" Alana inquired.

"How's tomorrow?"

13 · SURGE OF SATISFACTION

I WAS ON MY way to meet Simone for a meeting in Evanston when my cell phone rang. "Todd" flashed across the console, so I quickly flipped the phone open.

"Hey, baby," I said.

"What are you doing?" Todd asked in a playful, sexy voice.

"On my way to a meeting with Simone. What are you doing?" I asked with equal playfulness.

"Heading home. I forgot to grab my shirts for the dry cleaner and I am on my last one."

I loved that my man was so self-sufficient and not one of those men who always had to have their woman do everything domestic.

"While you're there can you grab my black pants suit and add it to your order?" I asked in a soft, pleading voice.

"I guess I could. What am I getting out of it?" Todd continued with his seductive voice.

"Well, you'll just have to wait and see tonight."

"I like how that sounds. So how's your day going?" he asked.

"Good, oh, I forgot to tell you, I hired Alana today."

There was dead silence on the phone, so long I thought Todd and I had been disconnected.

"Todd, did you hear me?"

"You hired Alana?"

"Yeah."

"My Alana?" he quickly added.

Todd's comment sent a surge of irritation down the back of my neck.

"Yes, I hired your Alana."

"For what?" he asked.

"To be the model on the campaign Simone and I are doing."

"Why would you hire Alana?"

"Well, she is a model, isn't she?" I asked.

"I don't understand, you don't even like her," Todd said as the irritation in his voice rang clear.

"That's not true."

"Yeah it is."

"Maybe I'm trying to make an effort," I countered.

"An effort for whom?"

"You, me, our relationship, I mean, come on, Todd. It's obvious that she isn't going anywhere anytime soon, so why not try to make an effort to get along with her?"

"But you don't like her," Todd said again, this time with a snappier tone.

I was starting to get irritated with Todd's accusations; he was making it seem like Alana and I were Biggie and Tupac.

"Okay, for the record Todd, I never said I didn't like her, I simply said that I didn't like her in our space all the time."

"Which translates to, you don't like her," Todd insisted.

"Why are you making such a big deal about all of this," I asked. "I'm trying to make peace and you're not even trying to meet me halfway."

"Because it's stupid that you hired her," Todd said, half shouting.

I was two seconds from hanging up on his ass. "Why are you so mad about me hiring Alana," I challenged him. "Are you sure there isn't something going on?"

I heard a pissed off chuckle on the other end of the line, proof that I knew how to turn the tables on his ass real quick.

"Kai, I don't know what I have to do to convince you that nothing is going on between Alana and me. I mean fuck, do I have to get it tattooed to my damn forehead?"

By now I had the phone at least five inches from my ear, having concluded that the conversation wasn't important enough to bust my eardrum.

"Whatever Todd, I'm just trying to bond with her since clearly she is your best friend in the whole wide world – and not going anywhere anytime soon," I repeated with extra sarcasm in my voice. I knew Todd hated that more than Whitney singing a capella.

"Fuck it, do whatever you want." Click. The phone went dead. I closed my cell phone and for the first time in days, I felt a surge of satisfaction.

14 · LIGHTS, CAMERA, ACTION

MY PLAN WAS WORKING great, actually better than I'd thought it would. My positioning Alana to work with us to get her from spending way too much time with my man? Priceless.

A whole month had passed, our campaign was taking off, and Alana was busier than ever. Todd finally came around after a few days of the silent treatment. When he did finally utter a word, he apologized for going off the deep end, blaming the stress of starting a new practice. I knew it had nothing to do with his practice, but I accepted his apology anyway.

Surprisingly, Alana was doing a fantastic job. Simone and I hired a fitness trainer for her and she dropped 10 pounds in the first month, seven in the second. I had to admit, standing at our photo session, watching Alana work her magic, I couldn't have picked a better model from the agency. Some would call it the luck of the draw.

I call it strategic placement.

I walked over towards Alana and our photographer, Conrad. We were shooting for a spread in W magazine and, well, Conrad Clark was the man to get that amazing shot.

"She definitely has a knack," Simone said, walking up behind me.

"That she does," I said in agreement.

"Thank your lucky stars," Simone said. I knew exactly what she meant. We had taken a chance on hiring Alana; thank God she was able to pull it off.

"What are you doing here?" I inquired.

"I came to see how your new project is coming along."

I knew Simone was talking about my newfound solitude with Todd. "Perfect," I said with a smile.

"Sounds like someone is getting more than her fair share."

"Let's just say our relationship couldn't be better."

"That's what I like to hear." Simone said.

"Hey, you wanna go grab a drink with me and Alana later?"

"Can't," Simone replied. "I have to find a model for the sample project coming up in the summer."

"I thought you had one already."

"I thought I did too," Simone said, "but when I saw the model they sent over I quickly let them know if I had wanted a snapping turtle I would've called the local zoo."

I shook my head and thought, "That's my friend." Then I looked over at Simone and said, "Well, I'll call you later."

"Ciao," she said as she gave Alana a wave and headed out the studio.

I looked back over at Alana and our eyes met just long enough for me to give her an approving nod. Alana quickly acknowledged her work well done before turning back towards the camera, giving Conrad her best pose yet.

•

Alana and I were finished with the shoot around four and

within an hour were sitting having drinks.

We usually go to "Pete's," a sports bar down the street from my office. It can get pretty busy, but I like the ambience and the fact that you can catch a game if you want.

I suggested getting together every Thursday for happy hour to sort of bridge the gap in our so-called relationship, not to mention to find out what Alana Brooks was all about. But our get-to-know-you sessions quickly turned into a weekly ritual that we both looked forward too, as we soon discovered how much we actually had in common.

I sat across from Alana at a window table sipping on my chardonnay. Alana was drinking her favorite, an apple martini, and I couldn't help stare at her and laugh right at that moment. There I was, hanging out with the same woman who had practically turned my world upside down just a few months prior. I chuckled to myself thinking, "Was I that insecure?" Yep, I sure was – and I wasn't ashamed to admit it, not at all.

I picked up my glass of wine and raised it high.

"Here's to a great photo shoot today," I said.

Alana grabbed her drink as well, and held it close to mine.

"And many, many more to come in the future," Alana added.

We clinked our glasses and took our sips.

I looked back up to notice Alana staring at me.

"What?"

"I really like your style Kai, not to mention I think you are very beautiful."

"Wow, well thank you?" I said as I shifted in my seat a bit. I don't know why It was hard for me to take a compliment, and doubly hard for some reason to take it from Alana.

"So how is Todd?" Alana asked as she played with her hair.

"He's good," I said.

"It feels like I haven't seen him in forever."

"That's because you've been busy honey, being a model," I

said with confidence.

"This is true," Alana said with excitement in her voice.

Alana and I held a stare, neither of us knowing what to say in that moment, and for the first time I felt a weird connection between us, although I couldn't quite put my finger on it.

"So how is Riley doing?" I asked.

"She is great, but growing up too fast. She'll be two soon."

"Well," I said, "this campaign is almost over so you can spend some more time with her."

"I can't tell you how thankful I am that you gave me this opportunity," Alana said. "I mean, I never thought I'd be modeling again after having a baby."

I wanted to say, "You wouldn't have been. Coveting one's boyfriend will get you ahead every time – well at least in the modeling industry, that is." But what I did say was, "Well Alana, the universe works in mysterious ways."

Alana took another sip of her drink. "Yes, it does," she said. "I mean, who knew we would click like we did?"

"Yeah, who knew?" I agreed.

"And the craziest thing is I look at you more as a friend than my boss."

"Thanks, I appreciate that," I said with a smile. I cleared my throat, as I felt a bit uncomfortable for that moment, with a real need to say what I was about to say. I didn't know if it was the wine talking but I had to get it out.

"I have to be honest with you, Alana, I was a bit, well, bothered by your friendship with Todd in the beginning."

"I could tell," she said, "and I don't blame you, but you have to know that Todd really loves you, a lot."

"I know, but I also realize I will never be able to replace you as his childhood friend."

"Todd considers you his best friend," Alana said.

"But he tells you more about what's going on in his life than he does me."

"That's because I'm not sleeping with him," Alana replied.

"You know men, they never want to reveal everything to the woman they hand over their heart to, it takes time for that, I mean, come on, they just mastered putting the toilet seat down, so it's one step at a time."

We shared a laugh.

"Yeah, I guess you're right," I added.

I finished off the rest of my wine, and then something came over me, something that even shocked myself.

"Maybe I'll call Todd to join us for a drink," I said, pulling out my cell phone.

"Good idea," Alana said. "It would be nice to see his big head."

As I dialed Todd's number, for the first time in ages I no longer felt powerless when it came to Alana and her relationship with Todd. I was in control and wanted to express it wholeheartedly.

It felt good.

A half hour later, Todd was sitting with us at Pete's having drinks, and there we were, the happy threesome, and I was able to breathe again - without the aid of a brown paper bag. And, for the first time since Alana strolled into my life, I felt that everything – everything – was going to be just fine.

15 · VOICES IN THE NIGHT

"LEAVE ME ALONE!" I screamed.

I tried to run but they blocked my way, one even pushed me down. Fear engulfed me. They stood over me and laughed, and laughed. My heart pumped faster and faster, my body was sore and dirty. I looked to the left, then to the right, plotting my escape. They kept laughing, high-fiving each other as if they'd done something great, but they hadn't. I wondered what I'd done to deserve this. My mind raced, I felt weak, cold, and confused, but they just kept laughing and taunting. I screamed again, this time loud enough to wake me from my bad dream. Todd jumped up and grabbed me.

I couldn't stop crying.

"Baby, it's a dream, it's just a dream," Todd said softly.

Todd's words had a way of pulling me back into reality and out of my hell. I stared at him, slowly waking up, slowly realizing that it was a dream. My body was wet from sweat and I felt a cold chill shiver through my whole being. I took a deep breath, pulled the covers back over me, and lay my head on Todd's shoulder.

"Is it the same one?" he asked softly as he rubbed my arm.

"Yes."

"Do you want to talk about it?"

"No," I whispered.

Todd was quiet, because he knew my dreams were something I wasn't ready to discuss in detail and he understood why.

We both slowly lay back down, Todd first, making himself a human pillow as I lay on top of him. Todd stroked my hair as I slowly began to drift back to sleep, but then my phone rang, waking me up. I glanced over at the clock – it was 3am – and clicked on the light. Todd sat up as I grabbed the ringing phone.

"Hello," I said in my Kermit the Frog voice.

"Hey, sis, you busy?"

"It's not a good time, Raymond."

"I didn't mean to call you so late, but I didn't know what else to do."

•

Twenty minutes later, I met Raymond in Grant Park on Columbus Drive, near Buckingham Fountain. It was cold as I walked hunched over, watching as my breath created a fog in front of my face. I walked towards a man sitting on a park bench, a bit slumped over. As I got closer I saw that his face was bruised and his mouth was bleeding. I then realized that the man was my brother.

"Oh my God, Raymond, what happened?" I exclaimed, sitting down next to him. I lifted his head to see the bruises a bit closer.

"I got into a little bit of an altercation, sis."

"With who?"

"Ah, it doesn't matter," Raymond said as he looked back down at the ground.

"What do you mean it doesn't matter," I asked. "Your nose looks like it's broken." I pulled out a tissue from my purse and tried to wipe the blood from his face.

"That's nothing," Raymond said. "It's my ribs that are really bothering me."

I looked down to see my brother holding his stomach. I went to move his arm and he winced in pain.

"I have to get you to the hospital," I told him.

"I don't need to see a doctor, sis, I just need a little bit of money to get by for a few more days."

I couldn't believe what I was hearing. My brother was sitting in the middle of Grant Park at 3:30am, with a broken nose and fractured ribs, and all he wanted to do was get high.

"Raymond, I'm not giving you money to get high, I'm taking you to the hospital."

Raymond stared at me without saying a word; he knew I was right, but he was also an addict and addicts have a one-track mind.

I ended up staying in the Emergency Room with Raymond until 7am. I called Todd so he wouldn't worry. I ended up falling asleep while they were treating him, only to awake to find that he was gone. They said Raymond slipped out without anyone noticing. The nurse looked at me, as if she'd seen it a thousand times.

"I'm sure he loves you, but he loves the drugs more," the nurse said as she handed me an invoice. I looked down to see that Raymond had racked up a hospital bill of over $3,000.

16 · BOREDOM BECOMES ME

TODD WAS OUT OF town for the weekend at a lawyers' conference so I was flying solo for the first time in our relationship. It felt weird, because ever since we'd started dating we had never been apart, especially after we became roomies, but I figured I could use a little "me" time.

I decided to relax, throw on some Miles Davis, take a long bath, and maybe even pamper myself with a mani/pedi and a hydrating facial mask. Work was beginning to stress me out and I needed some de-stressing right about then, and since sex was out of the question, I thought I'd better break out the Kai Edwards night spa.

My bath water was running when I heard the phone ring. Not really in the mood to talk, I grabbed it thinking that it was probably Todd wanting to say goodnight before he jumped in bed – but to my surprise it was Alana.

"Hey you, what are you doing?" Alana's voice was relaxed and sexy, as if she were having a spa night of her own.

"Just about to run a bath and jump in," I said.

"That sounds relaxing," Alana said.

"Yeah, It's been a long week."

"So what's up after your bath?" Alana asked with a twinge of anticipation in her voice.

"Manicure, pedicure, maybe a nice hydrating mask," I said.

"So I take it your in for the night?"

"Yeah, girl, I think I am," I replied.

"You up for some company?" Alana inquired.

Honestly, I wasn't in the mood for company, but Alana was different, and there was something about her energy that made her visits fun and comfortable.

"Where's Riley?" I inquired.

"My mom took her for the weekend, so like you, I'm flying solo, so I figured we could have a girls' night in. I can bring drinks and a movie."

All of a sudden my night of pampering sounding pretty boring and spending it with Alana seemed more intriguing.

"What the hell, come on over, I can order us some sushi and it should be here by the time you arrive," I said.

"Great, then I will see you in like an hour?" Alana shot back.

"Sounds like a plan," I said as I hung up the phone, still thinking that I should take a bath – I mean, come on, the bath water was already filled. No use in wasting my fifteen-dollar bath beads that were slowly dissolving and filling the room with a delicious and invigorating scent.

Alana arrived an hour later, on the dot. I ordered enough sushi for five, but that's just how I did it, since my eyes had always been bigger than my stomach and I loved variety. Alana brought over the ingredients for our drink of the night: a can of frozen pink lemonade, a bottle of Sprite, a small bottle of vodka, and whipped cream. Blend that up in a blender and you have an amazing drink called Pink Panties.

I was putting the food out as Alana started making the drinks. She was wearing a pair of Lucky jeans and a white v-neck t-shirt that she'd accessorized with a chunky pink and turquoise necklace and oversized rings. Flip-flops were her shoes of choice, mainly because on photo shoots I had her in three- or four-inch heels most of the time.

Alana had always been a beautiful girl to me, but something was different about her tonight. Something made her seem more, well, appealing. I found myself staring at her while she measured just the right amount of vodka; I couldn't believe what great friends we had become. I thought back to why I pulled her into my life, which was to keep her closer to me and off Todd's radar. My insecurities always got the best of me, and I hated it, but that was who I was. But all in all, I believed that everything happens for a reason, and for Alana and I to have become so close, so quickly, and have so much in common, it seemed like it was just meant to be.

"What?" Alana asked me, looking up.

"Huh?" I was quickly snapped out of my trance by the sound of her voice.

"Why are you staring at me, am I doing something wrong with the drinks?" Alana asked.

"Oh, um no, not at all, I was just thinking," I said quickly.

"About?" Alana asked as she turned back towards the blender to continue measuring and pouring the ingredients for our drinks.

"Just that I'm glad you came over tonight, that's all."

"Oh, no problem, besides, I didn't have a date tonight," Alana laughed.

"Oh, I see, you're just using me because you're ass is dateless."

"That's not true. I wouldn't do that," Alana said.

"Sure you would," I joked back.

"Okay, maybe."

We laughed again.

"What happened to Derrick? I thought you two were doing good."

"'Were' is the key word."

"What happened?" I asked.

"That brother was just too damn cheap, and to me, that is a huge turn off. Now don't get me wrong, he can work a sista out in the bedroom, but a cheap brother is just unattractive."

"Oh, I understand, that's one thing I love about Todd, he's never been cheap."

Alana stopped and turned to me.

"With you!" Alana exclaimed.

"Me?"

"In college Todd was the cheapest brother on campus."

"Are you serious?" I asked.

"One time I was so broke and Todd was the only one who had a job, so one night he went to Popeye's and ordered a three-piece dinner, came home, and ate it right in front of me – and wouldn't even share."

"Not even a chicken wing?"

"Nada, so like I said, he isn't cheap with you, and honestly, you're the first girl I've seen him like that with," Alana said.

"Really"

"Yep."

I listened to Alana talk about her memories with Todd and I had to admit, it did make me jealous – because she had history with a man that I truly loved, a man that I wanted to have history with, a man that I wanted to tell stories about.

•

By 10:30pm we were full, content, and close to tipsy. Those damn Pink Panties had a way of creeping up on us. Alana brought over the movie Kissing Jessica Stein; I had never seen the movie but had heard all about it. Basically it was about a straight woman who couldn't find love with the opposite sex so she found it with the same sex. Alana clicked off the TV.

"So what did you think of the movie?" Alana asked as she turned towards me, crossing her legs Indian-style on the opposite end of the couch.

"I liked it," I said.

"What did you like most about it?" Alana asked.

"Well, I liked how the movie didn't really portray her as gay, but as a woman looking for companionship, not really caring what the sex was, basically she was just open," I said.

"Yeah, I liked that too, so did you see that movie relating to your life at all?" Alana asked.

"What?" I replied.

"Did you see any similarities to your life?" Alana repeated.

Relating to my life? Similarities? I didn't know how to take that question – how would a woman who was involved with another woman have any similarity to my life?

"I don't know what you're asking me, Alana."

Alana gave me a look, took a sip of her drink, and slowly leaned in to me.

"Have you ever kissed a woman, Kai?"

That was the last question I thought would come out of Alana's mouth. Why would she even think that I had ever kissed a woman; I'm with Todd and I don't think I give off that gay vibe.

Or do I? I wondered.

"Why would you ask me that?" I inquired, trying not to sound too freaked out.

"Because it's the 21st century, and there are tons of women out there who fantasize about kissing a woman, so I was just wondering if you were one of them."

"A woman who fantasizes or a woman who has actually done it?" I tried to clarify.

"Well, now that you broke it down, both," Alana said.

"Well, I think we've all thought about it once or twice, it's human nature to be curious about some things."

"So is that a 'yes,' Kai?"

I stared at Alana for a moment. "Yeah, I have."

"Interesting, I never would have thought that."

"Thought what?"

"That you had 'those' thoughts."

"It's not like I think about it all the time, but it has crossed my mind – maybe once."

I was starting to feel a little uncomfortable with this conversation, not really knowing where Alana was trying to take it. I needed to do a bit of shifting. "Well, have you?" I asked, trying to throw the question back in her lap to see how she liked it.

"Have I what?"

"Have you thought about kissing a woman?" I asked.

"I've not only thought about it, I've actually been intimate with a woman," Alana answered, as if it were a no brainier.

"Really?" I replied, shocked.

The night had suddenly taken a turn in a direction that I would have never have thought possible. Alana had opened up Pandora's Box and at that moment I wanted to know more, much more.

"When did this happen?" I asked.

"About five years ago, I was on the road with a local modeling troupe out of Nebraska, her name was Tiffany, and she was sexy as hell."

"How did it happen?" I asked, hoping Alana would continue, hoping she didn't pick up the anticipation in my voice.

Alana sat back into the couch, took a sip of her drink, and looked away as if trying to remember the details of her story.

"Well, we had been on tour for a few months and I always thought she was very pretty, but never thought that much about it until one evening after a show, when she came to my hotel room. Now this woman exuded sex appeal like no one I had ever met, and I always felt something different about her but couldn't put my finger on it. Tiffany looked at me in a way that was different, exciting. So that night when she came into my room, I knew something was going to happen."

"Like what?"

"Like more than talking about tomorrow's fashion show."

I couldn't believe what I was hearing; Alana had been intimate with another woman? I wondered if Todd knew this, and if so, why the hell he hadn't told me.

"So what happened next?" I asked as if on the edge of my seat, as if I had just dropped $12.95 to see the next blockbuster hit. My excitement on the subject surprised even me, and I really didn't know why.

"That's something that I will take to my grave," Alana said as she smiled, then got up from the couch.

"What, where are you going?" I asked. I couldn't believe that Alana took me there but didn't deliver on the goods.

"We need another round of Pink Panties," Alana said as she grabbed my empty glass from the cocktail table along with her own, and headed to the kitchen.

I sat on the couch trying to imagine Alana kissing another woman; I never would have thought she would do something like that. I couldn't believe how curious I was; I really wanted to know what happened in that hotel room. I jumped up from the couch and headed to the kitchen, Alana was blending up a new batch of drinks. I hit the off button on the blender.

"Why did you do that?" Alana asked.

"Because you can't just keep me hanging, I need to know just what happened that night between you and Tiffany."

Alana smiled, turning towards me.

"You really want to know, huh?"

"Yes. You got me all curious," I said.

Alana gave me a seductive look.

"So why do you want to know so badly, Kai? Is it something that makes you excited?" Alana asked, and then stared deep into my eyes as if fishing for her own answer.

I started to feel uneasy; I didn't know why I was so interested, why I wanted to know so badly.

"Maybe," I said, not really knowing why that came out of

my mouth. My heartrate was accelerating.

"Maybe, huh?" Alana asked.

"Maybe," I said again, although repetition was a sure sign of nervousness on my part.

Alana finished the drinks and poured herself a glass, then me. She walked over towards me, both glasses in hand.

"Okay, if you really want to know what happened I'll tell you."

Alana handed me my drink. I took a quick gulp hoping the alcohol would shoot through my body and give me the liquid courage I needed to finish this encounter. Alana took a few sips from her glass as well, then gently took my drink out of my hand and set it on the counter. Her stare was a bit more intense, direct, and different. I didn't know what to think of it, but for some odd reason, I was wet.

"That night when Tiffany came into my room, she told me that she was extremely attracted to me. And then from the moment she saw me, she knew she had to have me. She knew that our chemistry would be off the hook – and it was."

"Really?" I asked.

"Yeah, and you know what I did, Kai?

"What?"

Alana leaned in close, so close I could smell the Pink Panties on her breath. "I kissed her, like this."

The next thing I knew Alana and I were in a serious lip lock, and I couldn't even tell you what happened between her saying "like this" and finding us in a sensual, passionate kiss that felt like it lasted for hours. In that moment, I was having an out-of-body experience.

Alana pulled away and just stared deeply into my eyes, not missing a beat.

"And that night, Tiffany and I shared what was the most amazing kiss ever, although I think our kiss was just as amazing. What do you think?"

I was speechless, not knowing what to say, but knowing I

wanted more. I found myself frozen in time, trying to piece together the steps that led up to that kiss, that unexpected but passionate kiss.

Alana kept her eyes locked on me as she slowly put her hand on the small of my back and pulled me in close to her. Our bodies touched as our lips connected and a small warm feeling filled my body. Alana's lips were soft and sensual, and I tasted all of what she was offering me with her tongue. Alana then leaned her body against mine as we fell back against the wall. I felt her hand move down my stomach, past my belt and right in between my legs. I let out a moan of passion as we continued to exchange a deep intimate kiss and Alana massaged that part of me that made me weak. In that moment nothing else mattered, nothing but my connection with Alana.

The phone rang, shattering our moment. I pulled away as I looked at the console; it was Todd.

"Shit!" I quickly grabbed the phone as a surge of guilt raced through my entire body. "Hey, baby," I said as I looked over at Alana. She gave me a smile, picked up her drink, and headed back to the living room.

"Hey beautiful, what are you doing?" Todd asked.

A question that was usually answered with great ease now gave me some difficulty.

"Nothing, really, just watching a movie," I said. I couldn't believe how that lie just rolled out of my mouth, although technically, I was watching a movie earlier. Todd knew that I hung out with Alana, but for some reason that night, I felt that he would read more into it, rightly so.

"Cool, what movie?" Todd asked.

Another trick question. I swallowed hard, searching for a movie, but my mind was coming up blank.

"Thomas Crown Affair," I said, cringing as I voiced the word "affair."

"Again? Baby, you're obsessed with that movie. How many times have you seen it?" Todd asked.

"Too many times," I said as I laughed with him. "So what are you doing up so late?" I was trying to take the focus off of me.

"Just got back from my meeting and I'm beat. I can't wait to get in bed."

"Well, then, you should go to bed, and I will call you in the morning," I said.

"Are you okay? You sound a little weird," Todd said.

"I'm fine, just kind of tired too, y'know?"

"Okay, well I'm going to hit the sack. Call you tomorrow?" Todd asked.

"Sounds good."

"Love you," Todd said.

" I love you, too."

I hung up the phone, took a deep breath, grabbed my drink, and headed back to the living room. Alana was lying on the couch. Her look was different, seductive almost. I knew at that moment that I had to regroup. "I, um, I have to go to the bathroom."

"Are you okay?" Alana asked as she sat up.

"I'm good," I said as I headed to the bathroom.

I sat there, in the bathroom, not knowing what to think of what had just happened, what to think of Alana, what to think of myself.

Twenty minutes later Alana knocked on the door. "You okay, Kai? You've been in there for a while."

"I um, I think I drank a little too much. Maybe we better call it a night."

"You sure?" Alana asked.

"Positive. I'll give you a call tomorrow," I shouted through the door.

There was silence on the other side, then, "Okay, well, I'll just let myself out."

"Okay," I said quickly.

I then heard footsteps and, finally, my front door opening and closing. I breathed a sigh of relief knowing that Alana was gone.

17 · UNWANTED COMPANY

SIMONE AND I WERE on a tight deadline for our campaign and I couldn't concentrate. All I could think about was what had happened the previous night with Alana. Todd would be home from the conference tonight and I couldn't get it out of my mind that I kissed his best friend – and that it felt good. My past thoughts about being with a woman were just that, thoughts; never once did I anticipate acting upon them.

Then again, I was never put in a situation where I was so tempted, either.

I was deep in thought when a knock at my door brought me back to the present. I looked up and there stood Alana. I hated that she was here; I wasn't ready to see her yet. Of course, I had to remind myself that I was the reason that she was here in the first place, since I hired her.

Alana looked even more beautiful than the last time I'd

seen her. Her make-up and her hair was perfect. She was look-ing exceptionally tempting in a white sundress which accented her figure perfectly.

I looked at my desktop and instinctively jumped into pro-fessional mode. I wasn't ready to deal with last night, especially not at the office.

"Hey, I'm glad you stopped by," I said quickly. "I wanted to brief you on your shoot today. It's with Sol magazine so I need you there by one and make sure you..."

Alana closed the door behind her and walked over next to me. "I can't stop thinking about you," she said, cutting me off.

Her words had always had a way of stopping me cold in my tracks. I tried to ignore her.

"Did you hear me, Kai?" she asked as she stood in front of me. "I can't stop thinking about you."

"Alana, I can't do this," I said as I looked up at her.

"Do what?"

"This – us, what happened last night – it's insane," I said. "I have a boyfriend so whatever this was, it has got to stop and it has to stop now, do you understand?"

"So you're saying you didn't enjoy last night?" As she moved closer to me.

"I'm, I'm not saying that, I'm just saying that this isn't right."

Alana and I held a stare, then something happened, an irresistible magnetic force came over me, Alana pulled me into her, and we kissed passionately. My heart was racing and I was lost – again.

My intercom buzzed and I quickly jumped three feet back. My secretary informed me that Todd was here.

"Here?" I said quickly, confirming the unexpected mes-sage.

"Yes, here," my secretary repeated. And before I had a chance to respond again, Todd was entering my office. Thank God for secretaries.

"Hey, baby!" Todd's voice sent a surge of lightning through my whole being.

"Hey, hey, baby, what are you doing here? I thought your flight didn't get in until tonight," I said a bit nervously as I made my way toward him.

I felt my nose, neck, and forehead breaking out in a cold sweat. I swallowed hard as I gave him a convincing welcome home kiss.

"The conference ended early and I wanted to get home."

"Wow, well, that's great," I said as I cleared my throat.

"Are you okay? You look a bit flushed," Todd said, staring at me.

"No, I'm good, just under a bit of stress from this project," I said.

"How about I take you to lunch at your favorite spot?"

"Wow, baby, that's sweet of you. What brought this on?" I asked, actually not knowing what else to say, but knowing it was because he missed me.

"I don't know, maybe I just missed you," Todd said in his sweetest voice.

Todd kissed me on the cheek and the guilt I felt earlier quickly intensified tenfold.

"Hello, Mr. Daniels," Alana said, interrupting our moment.

Todd looked around me to see Alana sitting over on my office sofa, and stepped to the side to greet her. "Hey you," Todd said.

Right then, in that moment, I couldn't help but feel that familiar feeling of jealousy rearing its ugly head again.

"Hello again, Mr. Daniels," Alana sang out.

"What are you doing here? Oh that's right, you work here now, you're a 'suuuupermodel," Todd playfully.

"Hey, don't hate," Alana shot back. "Appreciate the beauty that stands before you."

"Oh, I'm not hating, and I'm certainly not appreciating either," Todd continued jokingly.

"Whatever, Todd," Alana said as she walked over to us, bypassing me to give Todd a welcome home hug.

"Hey, I have an idea, why don't we all go to lunch?" Todd suggested.

"Perfect, I'm starving," Alana said as she shot me a quick wink.

I bit my bottom lip, then said, "Sure, that works for me," with a convincing smile.

As I watched Todd and Alana interact, my guilt from the night before slowly started to dissipate. I couldn't believe that I was still jealous of their friendship, their relationship.

Only now my jealously ran both ways.

18 · BREAKFAST IN BED

IT WAS 6AM ON Friday morning and I was up making eggs, waffles, turkey bacon, and coffee. I couldn't sleep, had a lot on my mind. So as a distraction for myself, I decided to surprise Todd with breakfast in bed. I figured since I did kiss his best friend, I would just shower him with affection to help subdue my guilt and make things right again. So I turned on some cool jazz and Martha Stewart'ed my way around the kitchen.

I was in the middle of scrambling four eggs with mush-rooms, green peppers, and cheese when the phone rang. I couldn't imagine who would be calling me so early on a Sunday. I glanced at the caller ID to see my parent's number and knew immediately it was my mother.

"Hello, darlin'," my mom sang into the phone.

"Morning, Corrine, what are you doing up so early?" I asked.

My mother hated when I called her by her first name, which I did from time to time. I always told her it was her own fault for sending me to those Montessori schools where the teachers insisted that we call them by their first names, so I figured it was okay with my mother as well.

"Sweetheart, I wanted to call you to let you know that I am having a dinner party next Saturday, and I'd like it if you would bring your new boyfriend. What's his name again?""Todd," I said.

"Say again?"

"Todd," I said again

"Spell that, honey."

"Todd, T-o-d-d, Todd."

"Oh, Todd, I got it," my mother said.

I didn't know if Corrine was developing a hearing problem or if all her years of teaching Montessori school had made her extra anal-retentive.

I told my mom that Todd and I would be there on Saturday. I hung up the phone and thought to myself, I knew the day would come when I would have to introduce Todd to my family, and since I was shacking up with this man it was high time they all got to see what I was working with. I continued to cook, cell phone went off. I glanced at the message from Alana: Are you available for drinks tonight?

I quickly texted her back and let her know that I had plans. I sat my phone down and continued to cook when it went off yet again, and, again. Another text from Alana: Can I come?

One thing I had been learning about Alana was that she was not shy about inviting herself, anywhere, at any time. I knew what Alana was doing and I couldn't let her get the best of me. I didn't feel right about what had gone down and the longer I avoided her the better the chance that my guilt would fade away. I quickly texted her back: Sorry, business meeting, Call you later.

Still feeling guilty, I finished my breakfast preparation by

7:30pm. I proceeded to meticulously place my scrumptious creation on a silver serving tray and complete with the Chicago Tribune, and carefully balanced it as I slowly walked to the bedroom. Todd was still fast asleep. I set the tray down next to the bed and slid in next to him. His body was warm and soft and I loved the way he smelled in the morning. I didn't want the breakfast to get cold, but also didn't want to deliberately wake Todd up. So I did it on the sly – with my cold feet. I slowly slid my icy cold feet over to meet his legs and sure enough, the brother popped up like a corn kernel in a hot pan.

"Morning, baby," I said in a soft, sweet voice.

"Baby, your feet are cold as hell."

"That's because I've been up making you breakfast in bed."

Todd looked at me then slowly sat up and looked over at the dresser to see – sure enough – breakfast in bed.

"Wow, thanks baby! What did I do to deserve all this?" Todd asked,

I wanted to say, "Nothing, just me kissing Alana and feeling guilty about it."

"Can't a girl show her man just how much she adores him?" I demanded between kisses, as I covered Todd's neck then slowly made my way down his bare, caramel chest. I looked up at him and he was all smiles.

"Damn, Skippy, you can. I like how you think."

I continued to kiss his chest as I headed all the way down to please him.

"I bet you do," I said as I went to work on my man.

In that moment, my guilt was gone.

19 · FIRE AND DESIRE

I WAS RELAXING ON the couch in our apartment. It was half past nine and Todd was working in his back office. My mind drifted to that sensual close encounter with Alana in my office when Todd walked in. How could I have explained being in a serious lip lock with his best friend, the woman I supposedly could do without in our lives?

I was drifting in and out of sleep when my cell phone buzzed. I quickly grabbed it to read my new message from Simone: Don't forget your boards for Monday morning's meeting. I texted her back: Of course not, and threw my phone back down on the table. A few seconds later it went off again; Simone was notorious for blowing me up at night with her last-minute thoughts, or as she liked to say, "bursts of inspiration." I sighed and grabbed my phone again, but this time it wasn't Simone, it was Alana. I sat up as I read her message: Can I see you tonight, are you done with your business meeting?

Since my business meeting was just an excuse to avoid Alana in the first place, I was pretty much available, but I texted her back: Finished early but really tired. Think I'm gonna just go to bed.

I had successfully been avoiding Alana for a few days, hoping that I could casually sweep our experience all under the rug, along with the conflicted feelings I felt for her. Unfortunately, with each passing day my feelings for Alana or the guilt of our actions would not dissipate. I wanted to see her, but I knew in my mind that I shouldn't, I couldn't.

My cell phone went off again. My heart began to race, I felt trapped. This was unfamiliar territory for me as I always have a solution to problems confronting me. I didn't know what the fuck to do at that moent. I hastily grabbed my my phone, took a deep breath, and read Alana's message: I'm at the "W" hotel, meet me for a drink, I just want to talk.

I stood and began to pace back and forth in the living room, thinking about what I could say to Todd as to why I was leaving the house at 9:30pm. And even though it was a Friday night, I had not told Todd that I had any plans. I started typing back to Alana: I can't leave tonight, and Todd is still up. I stared at my message, then erased it. I wanted to go, but I knew it was for all the wrong reasons. My mind began to play devil's advocate, telling me to just go meet her for a drink, it wasn't that big of a deal.

Before I had a chance to text Alana back, she texted me again: Kai, don't think, just come. It was almost like she was reading my mind, and she was right, I was thinking way too much about the situation. I stared at her message and quickly typed back: I'm on my way. I hit "Send". Relief. I commited. I was excited to see her.

Then reality hit, and hit hard. What would I tell Todd?

I slowly walked toward his office and gently knocked on the half-open door. He looked up from his computer.

"Hey," he said softly.

"Hey."

"What's up, you going to bed already?" he asked.

"No, actually my brother just called me, he really needs to talk so I'm going to go meet him."

And there it was, a complete bald-faced lie in a very convincing tone. I hated lying to Todd, but I didn't know what else to do. I wanted to see Alana.

"Okay. How is he doing anyway?" Todd inquired.

"He's okay, you know, just taking one day at a time," I said.

"Tell him I said to keep his head up," Todd said.

"I will. You sure you don't mind me going?" I asked, feeling my guilt rise with each syllable that escaped from my mouth.

"Baby, it's cool, your brother needs you, so go, and I still have a few hours of work to do here," Todd said as he started shuffling the papers on his desk.

"Okay, so I'll be back as soon as I can," I said.

"Take your time," Todd replied.

"Thanks."

With that, I turned to leave, feeling a sense of relief, excitement and guilt. Then Todd said something that jilted the shit out of me. "Where are you meeting him?"

"Huh?"

"Where does your brother want you to meet him?" Todd asked again.

I was at a loss for words; I didn't expect Todd to ask me any specifics. I turned slowly back towards him, simultaneously thinking of another lie to tell.

"This, um, café over on Dearborn," I quickly said, thanking the Lord Jesus that I didn't stutter too much.

"Oh, okay. Well, be careful, make sure you take a cab. I don't want you walking this time of night."

"I will, baby," I said as I turned and walked back down the

hallway towards the front door.

As I grabbed my coat, I couldn't believe that I just lied to my man to go see a woman who I couldn't stop thinking about – a woman who was his best friend.

•

I arrived at the "W" hotel around 10pm, and as I walked into the lounge off the main lobby. My eyes immediately found Alana sitting at the bar alone. I felt nervous and excited all at once. I took a deep breath and headed over to where she was sitting. I always loved the W hotel. It always had a quaint and very sexy ambiace, and tonight it was all that and more. The lounge was seductively and dimly lit with soft candlelight. Smooth jazz softly filled the room. It was a slow night but not dead. A nice fix of people, business and social, filled the room sipping cocktails and engaged in pleasant conversation.

Alana sat at the bar sipping on a martini (my guess? apple, which was her favorite). She looked great. She was wearing a white skirt with a matching white tank top subtly accentuating her cleavage. Her hair was down and naturally curly.

"Hey, you," I said as I slid into the bar stool next to her.

"You made it!" Alana said with a broad smile on her face. She leaned over and planted a kiss on my cheek. "Thanks for coming?"

I couldn't help thinking how beautiful and sexy this woman was. And it was blowing my mind, because ever since we kissed she seemed even more beautiful and sensual than before.

"Can I buy you a drink?" Alana offered as she waved the bartender down.

"Sure, I'll take a white wine, thanks," I said as I tried to make myself comfortable.

"Coming right up." Alana ordered my wine then turned her bar stool and all her attention towards me.

"So I take it you've been busy, since I haven't heard from you in a few days," Alana said, as she looked me up and down with a seductive grin.

"Yeah, well about that, Alana," I said as I adjusted myself in my seat. I felt uncomfortable, as if just meeting her for the first time. "I guess I've been trying to deal with what happened, it really threw me for a loop, y'know?"

"Yeah, I figured as much, which brings me to the reason I asked you here tonight."

Alana turned and took a sip of her drink. Maybe she was just as nervous as I was, but she did not look it at all.

"Kai, I wanted to apologize for kissing you. I get caught up sometimes and, well, I'm sorry if I made you feel uncomfortable. It won't happen again."

I felt instantly deflated upon hearing Alana's words. I guess I hadn't expected her to throw in the towel so quickly. Truth be told, I wanted to kiss her again.

My attraction to Alana was real and even though I knew it was wrong, I couldn't deny it. But even worse, I couldn't bring myself to say what I was feeling, so I took another gulp of my wine, and as I placed my glass back on the bar, Alana placed her hand on my thigh.

"Unless, of course, you're not okay with that, Kai," Alana said as she gave me a look, a look that told me that she knew I wasn't.

My body immediately tensed up, and I couldn't speak. My words were stuck between my thoughts and my mouth. Alana smiled then leaned in close to me. "Can I tell you a secret, Kai?"

"Sure," I said, hesitantly.

"I have been attracted to you since the first day I met you. Remember? At the opening of Todd's firm?" Alana asked as she slid her hand slowly up my thigh.

I took a deep breath, breathing in all of her sensuality in that moment.

"You are so sexy to me and I admire your ambition, creativity and drive," Alana said as her hand continued up my thigh.

I felt my body temperature rising with each syllable she spoke. I wanted to kiss Alana so badly it was insane. I reached out and put my hand on top of her hand. Alana looked deep in my eyes again.

"I have a room upstairs."

"You do?" I said in a soft, almost muted voice.

"Do you want to come up?" Alana asked. She continued to rub my thigh as she moved in to caress my inner.

"I promise, no regrets," Alana said as she gave me one last smile. I was still speechless as I watched Alana quickly finish her drink, pay the bill, and stand. She gave me one last look as she turned to leave. I watched her for a few seconds as she headed out of the bar, realizing that she never waited for me to answer. I guess she knew I wanted to be with her just as bad as she wanted to be with me.

I downed the last of my wine like a 2 oz. shot before standing and quickly following Alana out the bar and up to her room.

20 · AN AFFAIR TO... FORGET

THE HOTEL ROOM WAS was dimly lit and smelled like sweet lavender. I sat nervously on the edge of the California king bed as Alana finished up in the bathroom. I ran my hand across the embroidered bedspread, taking in my surrounding as my mind raced.

I couldn't believe I was here, I glanced over at the clock, it was now 11:30pm and I wondered if Todd was thinking of me, wondering when I was coming home. I checked my cell phone to see if he had called, but no calls and no text messages from Todd. I guess I was in the clear – for now.

Alana opened the bathroom door and I immediately tensed up upon seeing her. I couldn't believe how nervous I was.

Alana headed towards the bed, stopping inches from me, and ran her fingers through my hair and down the side of my face. "I think you need another drink."

"Yeah, I think you're right," I said quickly, agreeing with her observation.

Alana turned and headed over to the bar and started making two drinks. I watched her from behind, thinking of how it would be to touch a woman, to be intimate for the very first time. My secret fantasy was about to be put to the test and I was nervous as hell.

I couldn't help but wonder if my attraction to Alana was a suppressed feeling or just something new that came over me since she had walked into my life. Either way, I wanted to explore more of this and I knew that now there was no turning back.

Alana brought my drink over then sat next to me on the bed.

"You okay?" Alana asked.

"I guess I'm a little nervous."

"That's understandable, I was hella nervous my first time."

"You?" I asked, surprised.

"Oh, yeah!" Alana said as she sipped on her drink. "But I was comfortable with the person I was with." Alana put her drink down, then looked into my eyes as she softly rubbed the side of my face with the back of her hand. "Are you comfortable with me, Kai?"

I looked at Alana for a minute, then said, "Yeah, I am."

"Good," Alana said as she slowly took my drink out of my hand and placed it on the bedside table. I felt my heart beating faster and faster as Alana reached out and touched my thighs, her hand sliding in between them as she slowly caressed them up and down. She then made her way up to my stomach and back down between my legs again. The room was quiet and all so still. I could hear my erratic breathing pass through my nose and mouth. My heart was pounding a mile a minute.

"Just relax, Kai, let me do all the work," Alana whispered as she leaned in and kissed me gently on my lips, then my

cheek, then softly rubbed the side of her face against mine. I
wanted to reach out and touch her, to feel her, but I felt paralyzed, thinking if I moved I would disturb her flow. I closed my
eyes as Alana slowly went down to kiss my neck, covering each
side equally, her wet tongue gliding up to my chin. I felt myself
getting wet as Alana's hand slid back between my thighs, this
time moving upward as she continued to kiss my neck softly. I
opened my eyes to see Alana looking at me and all I could
think in that moment was that I loved everything about her: the
smell of her hair, the smoothness of her skin, the feel of her soft
lips against my breast, neck, and face. I remembered thinking,
"I can't believe I'm kissing my man's best friend." That thought
alone should have made me stop and rethink how my actions
were creating the raw seeds of hurt, deceit, confusion, and pain
– but it didn't, not even for a second, because in that moment,
Alana's touch made the wrong feel right and the guilt act as if it
had no place in my consciousness. I was lost in her, hoping
never to be found, and desperately hoping the feeling was
mutual.

"Hey, you okay?" Alana said, pulling back.

"Yeah, I'm just enjoying being with you."

"Me, too," Alana whispered as she touched my face then
kissed me gently on my lips. Her mouth was soft as I felt her
tongue part my lips, sliding it against mine – and the moment I
kissed her back, I felt a sense of passion flow through my body.
An energy was connecting the two of us and I could once again
breathe.

I reached out for Alana as we slowly fell back on the bed.
Alana slowly crawled on top of me. I could feel her heart beating rapidly as her body pressed against mine. We continued to
kiss, and Alana caressed my entire body. She gently separated
my legs as she began to grind against me. I reached out and
pulled her closer as we moved together, back and forth.

I felt Alana reach for my shirt, and she pulled it up and
over my head. I reached behind my back to unhook my bra, but

Alana quickly stopped me. "I told you, let me do all the work," Alana said as she slid behind me and slowly unhooked my bra. It fell to the bed as she kissed the back of my neck as she began making her way down my spine and then back around to the front of me. I leaned back on my elbows as Alana started to unbuckle my jeans, working to pull them off as I lifted my pelvis up to help her – then suddenly she stood up, pulling them off with one motion.

I sat up but Alana slowly lowered me back on the bed and slid on top of me. She straddled her legs on both sides of me, and lowered her head to kiss my stomach. Her tongue felt delightful as it rounded my belly button before teasingly entering it and coming back out again. She continued downward, kissing my stomach as she caressed my spot with her hand through my panties. My breathing quickened, I was getting wetter with each touch, as her fingers slowly moved my panties to one side and her finger gently caressed my wetness.

Then before I knew it Alana was slowly sliding off my panties. I let out a sigh. Alana let out a moan as her mouth traveled down between my thighs, I couldn't help but to convulse every time she touched a sensitive spot. Alana continued to kiss my inner thigh and it sent a surge of pleasure and pain through my body. I arched my back and braced myself by grabbing hold of the side of the bed. Alana continued upward towards my golden brown triangle and I could feel my body temperature rising with each inch. Alana reached up to caress my breasts as her tongue worked my magic spot from all angles. I was now jerking and contorting uncontrollably like a fish out of water, screaming to be thrown back in. I peered down at Alana and was finally able to utter my first words, "Oh, God, Alana!"

Alana looked up. "How bad do you want it, baby?"

"Please... don't... stop."

Alana smiled a devilishly pleasing smile before diving back into my sea of wetness. I screamed, she moaned, as she moved up and down and back and forth. Her lips felt soft and wet against mine, her fingers moved in and out of me with ease. I was lost in carnal pleasure. Next, in one almost choreographed motion, Alana lifted up my leg, and flipped me over on all fours, as her tongue entered me from behind. My head started to pound from the intense pleasure I was experiencing. My legs became weak and my throat was dry as I steadily began to climb the ladder of ecstasy all the way to the top.

•

Oh shit!" I woke up screaming and jumped off the bed. I looked at the clock. It was 4:30am.

"What?" Alana said as she woke from her deep sleep. "What's wrong?"

"I have to go, I have to go home," I said, stumbling through the darkness of the room, trying to locate my clothes.

I saw Alana glance at the clock.

"Oh damn," Alana replied, half awake, half asleep. "Do you need me to cover for you or say anything to Todd?"

"No, I got it under control. I just didn't expect to fall asleep."

I quickly threw on my clothes, trying to piece my outfit back together in the dimly lit hotel room. I was feeling frantic, awkward and guilty all at once. I couldn't believe I feel asleep – in Alana's arms.

I said my goodbye with a quick peck on Alana's lips before running out the door and heading home to my man.

I arrived home just past 5am. The birds where chirping, and horizon was turning from deep blue to a fiery orange as the sun was beginning its ascent over Lake Michigan. I quietly slinked through the door I felt like I was in high school and coming home from a party I was forbidden to attend. My first stop was the bathroom as I did a quick wash up, hoping to eliminate the scent of Alana and our taboo indiscretions. I headed to the bedroom to find Todd fast asleep. I took a deep breath as I slowly quietly crawled in next to him; Todd turned and half-acknowledge my presence.

"Hey, how's your brother?" he mumbled.

"He's fine. Go back to sleep, baby, I'll tell you all about it in the morning."

"Okay," Todd said as he closed his eyes then wrapped his arms around me.

His sleepy embrace felt comfortable but right then, all I could think about was Alana.

21 · THE DAY AFTER

MY GUILT WAS STARTING to overwhelm me. It was equaled by my ever growing desire for Alana. I couldn't believe how conflicted I felt and it was killing me. I needed to talk to someone but at the same time I didn't know what to say, or even how to say it. I started to feel paranoid, thinking that everyone could tell that I just slept with a woman, almost as if it were stamped on my forehead for all to read, judge, and scrutinize.

It was noon and I sat in my favorite coffee shop waiting for Todd to arrive. We had a ritual of meeting there once a week for coffee since it was where we first met. Just my luck – our day happened to fall on the day after I slept with Alana. And since I had never missed a day, I couldn't miss today of all days.

I never did fall asleep that morning after leaving Alana and crawling into bed with Todd. I eventually just got up, took a shower and left the house before Todd got up, leaving him a note which said I had a few errands to run and I would see him at the café later on. I wasn't ready to see Todd yet, I wasn't ready to look into his face after I did the unthinkable: Slept with his best friend... A woman!

My head was pounding with confusion and excitement so I closed my eyes to grab a welcome little reprieve, but that was quickly interrupted when my cell phone started to ring. I grabbed it before the entire song ("Promiscuous Girl") played out. I definitely needed to change my ring tone, I thought.

"Hello," I said.

"Hey, you." Alana's voice sent an unexpected chill through my body.

"Hey."

"What are you up to?" Alana inquired.

"Waiting for Todd at the coffee shop."

"Oh." Alana was quiet; I'm sure the mere mention of Todd's name had a totally different meaning now than it did before.

"So Kai, I called to tell you that I had a really nice time with you last night and, well, I can't stop thinking about you."

I quickly looked around the café, making sure no one was in earshot. I hunched over as I dropped my voice down an octave to a whisper.

"I, um, I can't stop thinking about you either," I said.

"I want to see you again, Kai."

I took a deep breath upon hearing this. I didn't know how to digest it all. Everything was going way too fast.

"What about Todd?' I asked.

"What about him?"

"What if he finds out?"

"I thought about that," Alana replied, "and I know we're skating on thin ice here, but Kai, I don't want to stop seeing you. Are you having second thoughts?"

I contemplated Alana's question, and the crazy thing was, I

never once had second thoughts. Guilty thoughts, yes, but it never crossed my mind to stop seeing her.

"Kai, are you there?" Alana said, pulling me back from my racing thoughts.

"Yeah, I'm here, I'm just having a hard time with the guilt that's all," I said.

Then, before I knew it, I had an idea. And before I could stop it, it was shooting out of my mouth like a cannonball.

"Maybe we should tell him," I said.

"Tell who?"

"Todd."

"Are you crazy, Kai? He would kill us!" Alana exclaimed. "Listen Kai, if we continue to see each other, we have to promise that we will never, ever tell Todd."

"Yeah, you're right. I guess I thought if I got it off my chest I wouldn't feel so guilty."

"Yeah," Alana said, "but then you would have to deal with maybe breaking up your relationship and my friendship with him, which in my opinion is way more devastating than a little guilt. Believe me, it's better this way, Besides, Todd would never understand."

"No, he wouldn't," I agreed.

"Kai, this should be our secret. No one has to know but us, right?" Alana added.

I looked up to see a middle-aged woman staring my way, and wondered if she was eavesdropping in on my conversation. I shot her an evil look as I lowered my voice even more.

"Right."

"So then, we agree that we will never say anything to Todd," Alana said.

"Yeah, I promise."

So there you have it, that was our agreement and our pact – that Todd would never find out, at least not from either of us.

I hung up with Alana and continued to wait for Todd. Twenty minutes later I got a text message from him that he had an emergency at the office and had to go in to take care of it. In the past I would have been annoyed to the tenth power, but right then, at that very moment, I felt relieved. I wasn't ready to face my boyfriend; I needed a little more time to think. I quickly texted him back "No problem" then took a deep breath as I closed my eyes again, to finally grab that little bit of well-needed reprieve.

22 · A SECRET REVEALED

"WHAT IS GOING ON that you had to pull me out of my Sunday yoga class?" Simone asked as we sat in Pizza Capri at the height of the lunch rush.

"I have to tell you something," I said, feeling a bit uneasy as well as having a sense of urgency.

"What? What's wrong?" Simone asked, looking me dead in my eyes.

"It's, um, it's pretty devastating."

"Kai, what is it? You're scaring me."

I leaned forward to reveal my secret as well as relieve a small part of my guilty conscience. "I cheated on Todd."

Simone's body instantly relaxed as she fell back into her chair.

"Oh, girl, is that it? I thought someone died."

"I cheated on Todd with, with… Alana."

"Whoa," Simone said, as she sat right back up in a perfectly erect position. "You slept with Alana?"

"Yes."

"Our Alana?"

"Yes," I said.

"Wow!" Simone said as she slumped back into her chair.

"Yeah, wow," I said, echoing her sentiments. "So what are you thinking?" I asked, desperately needing to know what was on Simone's mind.

"I'm thinking that, uh, this is pretty damn hot, so keep talking and don't leave out any details."

"Simone!" I exclaimed.

"What? For once you pull me out of yoga class for something important. Not like last month when you needed me to take you to the hospital after you tripped over that stupid tree branch," Simone said.

"I thought I broke my ankle."

"That's what 911 is for."

"Can we please focus here?" I asked.

"Okay, sorry. So you and Alana, wow."

"Is that all you have to say? Not, 'I can't believe you cheated, let alone with a woman?'"

"No, you're right. At least tell me if she was any good," Simone said with a curious and intrigued grin.

"Simone!"

"What do you want me to say, Kai?"

"I don't know. Tell me I'm a bad person, tell me that you disapprove, something. I cheated on Todd with Alana!"

"Okay, first of all, you're not a bad person, because in the book of Simone, everyone cheats, and secondly I don't disapprove because frankly it's your life," she said.

"But aren't you even curious as to why I slept with her," I asked, "or for that matter, that I slept with a woman?"

"Kai, if you think I'm going to judge you, I'm not. No one has the right to judge anyone, we should all be able to live our lives the way we want to live them. My philosophy is just be fucking happy and if that means fucking your man's best friend, who is a woman, then so be it."

"Do you think I'm gay?" I asked. Although I didn't think that I was, I kinda needed to hear another person's opinion – Simone's opinion.

"I think you were curious and she's beautiful. Hell, after a few martinis I might have gone there, too."

We shared a laugh with that one.

I really didn't know how to take all of this, but for some odd reason I didn't feel as bad as I did five minutes before. I paused for a minute and thought back to that night, that night when Alana and I sleep together for the very first time.

"Thanks for that Simone, you just don't know how nervous I was telling you."

"Come on, it's me, Simone, your best friend, the woman who has been stripped of all her morals and then some. Honestly, I'd rather just hear how the sex was."

I sat back on my chair feeling very relaxed. I was so glad I had Simone in my life; she made me feel great whenever I felt like crawling in a cave and hiding for months.

"I do feel guilty though," I continued. "I don't know what came over me. I've never done anything like this in my life."

"We all do things we feel guilty about in our lives, but we can't let it ruin us. We're human, we all make mistakes."

"Human – that I am," I agreed.

"Let me ask you this," Simone said. "How did you feel being with her?"

"I don't know, I felt safe and comfortable, but then again, I feel the same way when I'm with Todd."

"Do you still love him?" Simone said.

"I do, with all my heart. And this thing with Alana will probably not happen again, I don't know what came over me."

"It happens to the best of us, believe me," Simone replied.

"So what about you, would you ever get with a woman?"

Simone sat back as she contemplated my question, a devilish smile crawling across her face. "Maybe, if she was the right woman I guess, I never really gave it much thought."

"How would you handle the guilt?" I asked.

"Honestly, I think I would have more guilt eating a piece of white bread than cheating on my husband with a woman."

We shared another good laugh with that one.

"So would you tell your husband then?" I inquired.

"Probably not."

"Really? Why?"

"Men can't handle it," Simone answered. "Some say they would love it if their woman got with another woman, they even go so far as to brag about it, but when it becomes their reality, they flip out. Happened to a friend of mine."

"What happened?"

"Let's just say it wasn't good."

Simone picked up her bottle of water and took a sip, then placed it back down on the table and crossed her arms across her chest.

"So my suggestion," Simone continued, "is to keep your little secret to yourself. Todd isn't ready for this one, not yet, especially since it involves Alana."

"Yeah, that seems to be the consensus," I said.

It turned out that Alana was right; my night with her would have to be our secret, one that we would have to keep from my man – forever.

23 · GUESS WHO'S COMING TO DINNER

"ALANA'S GOING TO MEET us for dinner," Todd said.

"What?" I asked as my head jerked up from my menu, hoping I hadn't heard what I know Todd had just said. "Alana?" I repeated, just making sure I'd heard him correctly.

"Yeah, Alana."

"But I thought we were going to have a quiet dinner, just the two of us," I said, pleading my case.

"I know, but she called me tonight and didn't have anything to do. I thought it would be nice to see her since it's been a while. Besides, you guys are friends now, right?" Todd asked as he stared at me, waiting for an answer.

"Right, yes we are, um, friends now," I said as I looked back down at my menu.

I felt instantly annoyed. There was still this unexplainable hold Alana had over Todd that I couldn't put my finger on, although I couldn't complain one freaking bit, since I was sleeping with her.

I took a deep breath. I could only wonder how it would feel to be sitting at the same table with Todd and Alana. What would we talk about? What if Todd saw right through our façade? What if I broke down?

"Are you okay?" Todd asked, pulling me out of my internal banter.

"Yes, why?"

"I don't know, you seem a little distracted."

"I'm fine. I've just got a lot on my mind with work right now," I said, looking down at my menu again but not really reading it.

"You want to talk about it?" Todd asked.

"Actually, I'm good, it's nothing that won't work itself out."

"Okay," Todd said as he looked back down at his menu, then back up. "I wonder what's taking Alana so long to get here?"

"Maybe she's stuck in traffic," I ventured, although I was really hoping that she wouldn't show up.

I had not seen Alana since we took our friendship to the next level, although it had only been a few days. I wasn't ready, not this soon. I was definitely avoiding her, trying to escape a situation like this one I'd gotten into.

I closed my menu and looked up to see Alana entering the restaurant.

"Finally, there she is," Todd said, spotting Alana the moment she walked through the glass doors.

"Great," I said, trying to mirror his enthusiasm. Alana saw us and headed our way. I wondered why she hadn't told me that she was meeting us for dinner. I felt like I was left in the dark, without any time to prepare, or to think of what to say or how to act. I've always hated being unprepared.

"Hey, you two," Alana said as she approached us with a huge smile on her face. Alana looked amazing and smelled equally as great. Todd stood and they gave each other a friendly kiss and a hug. Then it was my turn – my turn to act like the normal friend I was supposed to be. Alana turned towards me and I smiled and stood and gave her a pat-pat hug, then quickly sat back down. As Alana sat, she shot me a look and a quick wink. I didn't acknowledge it, but grabbed my menu to look over it – for the third time.

"So what's up, Ms. Alana? You look good," Todd proclaimed.

"Thanks, had a facial and a full body wrap today," Alana said.

"Hmmm, must be nice, I wish I could get a facial and a full body wax on a Monday afternoon," Todd joked.

"You could, you just choose not to," Alana threw back.

"Exactly," Todd said. "With my schedule, I'm happy if I get to eat."

"So how is the practice, Washington and McClendon, coming along?"

"Busier than ever, but it beats working for someone else," Todd said.

"And how long have I been on you about starting your own practice?" Alana asked.

"All right, all right, don't start. Yes, I finally took your advice, O Wise One."

"Wise One? I kinda like that," Alana said as she reached for the basket of bread.

I found myself silent as Alana and Todd exchanged their playful banter. I stared at both of them; they were both so beautiful to me, and I couldn't help but feel attracted to both of them in that moment. I began to wonder how it would be to have both of them at the same time, although when it came time for Todd and Alana to be intimate I'm not sure that it would sit well with me. Then again, I thought, I guess I had a lot of nerve seeing that I'd slept with both of them.

"So how are you doing, Kai?" Alana asked, ending my trance and directing all her attention toward me.

I stared into Alana's eyes and I saw more than a general question; I saw a stare that I had never seen from her before, a stare Todd used to give me when we first met, one full of intrigue and, if I wasn't mistaken, a little lust.

"I, um, I'm good. Simone and I are working on a new campaign and, well, it's coming along, since we have to get a few, or maybe it's just a couple, of clearances to make it happen. Not to mention the project that you're working on, but all in all everything is coming together."

I couldn't believe how long and drawn out I'd made that simple statement sound. I totally needed a drink.

"Well, that's the ad biz, right?" Alana responded with a smile.

"That it is," I answered.

"I don't know about you two, but I am starving," Alana said.

"Me too, so where is our waitress?" Todd added.

"Maybe you should go see what's taking our waitress so long," Alana said as she looked at Todd.

"That's a good idea. I'll be back," Todd said as he quickly jumped up, leaving Alana and me at the table, alone.

Alana turned to make sure Todd was out of earshot, then quickly turned back to me.

"I miss you," Alana said

"You do?"

"Of course, but clearly you don't feel the same."

"That's not true, I do, Alana, Why didn't you tell me you were meeting us for dinner?"

"Todd told me not to. He thought it would be his little surprise since he knows we're such close friends now. If only he knew just how close we are!" Alana said with a chuckle.

Then, to my surprise, Alana reached under the table and

touched my thigh, and a sweet sensation shot through my body.

"Alana," I said.

"What?"

"We're in a restaurant."

"No one can see me," she said as she began to caress my inner thigh. "I want to see you later, can we make that happen?" Alana asked as her hand moved up my thigh.

"I can't," I said, even though I wanted to. "What would I tell Todd?"

"Tell him the truth, that you're hanging out with me. He won't care. Besides, there's this new lounge I want to check out in Wicker Park called Blu." Alana gave me a seductive smile. "It's dark and quaint and…"

Todd's voice snuck up from behind. "You guys think you're fooling me, don't you?" My heart skipped a beat as Todd sat back down.

He stared at both of us for a few beats, then said, "I know what's going on, I'm not stupid."

"What are you talking about?" Alana said as she slowly slid her hand off my leg and casually leaned back in her chair.

I was at a loss for words. I looked at Alana and she looked at me.

Todd broke the silence. "You two are sitting over here trying to plan a surprise birthday party for me, but I told you, I'm not having it. I don't want it to be a big deal this year."

"See how much you don't know, Todd?" Alana said. "Kai and I were sitting here thinking of how we could ditch you tonight and check out this new lounge. We weren't thinking about your funky birthday."

"Oh, damn," said Todd. "I feel stupid."

"Yeah, ya should, but we still love you," Alana added

"Well, I'm headed out to watch the Bears game after this anyway, they're playing the redskins, so I was hoping you two would hang out," Todd said as he turned to me. "Is that cool with you, baby?"

"Yeah, sure, not a problem," I shot back. I couldn't believe how easy it was, almost as if it was meant to be.

"Cool." Todd said as our waitress walked up.

"Great, then let's order, "Alana said as she gave me a look and smile.

•

We parted after dinner, going our separate ways – Todd to his game, and Alana and I to our lounge. I was still a little shaken from our close encounter in the restaurant. I made it clear to Alana that we had to be extra careful in how we inter-acted with each other when Todd was around, and her putting her hand on my thigh was a definite no-no. Alana agreed, but quickly let me know that it would be hard for her since she was so attracted to me; she even threw in how sexy I could be as well. Even though those statements made me feel good, I told Alana that she needed to try harder.

We arrived at Blu around 9pm. The lounge was small and invitingly cozy. There was a satisfying aroma in the air of sweet lavender. The lighting was dim and sweet jazzy tunes floated through the air. The Blu lounge was distinguished by seating in the shape of beds attached to the walls where one could sit up right or stretch out completely and relax. I saw an open spot in the corner and we headed that way before anyone had a chance to snag it. We crawled in the bed/booth and quickly ordered up a round of drinks. I knew what I had told Simone, that my encounter with Alana was a one-time thing, but whenever I looked at her, I knew it would happen again, for sure.

"So how do you feel?" Alana asked, giving me a look, as if trying to decipher my thoughts.

"What do you mean?"

"Are you okay being here right now?"

"I came, didn't I?" I said.

Alana raised an eyebrow. "Okay, I see we're doing just fine then."

I glanced around the room, noticing the array of different people, couples, singles, all mingling and getting better acquainted. I wondered if I knew anyone here, and if so, if they would pick up on anything.

The waitress brought over our drinks. Alana handed me mine and after taking hers she then raised her glass.

"A toast, to friendship with benefits and an unspoken affair," Alana said with a devilish smile and a wink.

I couldn't believe that I was not only sleeping with my man's best friend but toasting to never uttering a word about it. It was definitely something I never could have imagined in a million years.

I then raised my glass high in the air, clinked it with Alana's and took more than a sip. I guess I was more than "okay" – I was celebrating it.

As the night progressed so did my buzz and I began to realize that my attraction to Alana was growing stronger with each drink. That got me wondering if my sexual attraction to her was alcohol-induced, or simply growing over time as I got more comfortable with her.

The lounge was getting a lot more crowded and I was getting way too tipsy, and I was ready to go home. I downed the last of my third glass of wine as I leaned into Alana.

"Are you about ready to go?" I asked, hoping she felt the same.

"Give me twenty more minutes, I kinda wanna dance. Let's go dance," Alana said as she started to groove, sitting down, to Chris Brown.

Dancing was the last thing on my mind. I was thinking more of napping.

"You go," I said. "I'm kinda tired."

"Okay, I'll be back," Alana said as she jumped off our booth/bed and disappeared in the sea of people. I lay back as I thought about Todd, wondering what he was doing, wondering if he was thinking about me. I couldn't imagine what he would

think or even do if he found out what was going on. I shook
the thought out of my head before driving myself crazy. I drank
the rest of my wine and continued to people-watch as I waited
for Alana to come back.

Some twenty minutes and five songs later, I looked up to
see Alana heading back my way with a guy in tow. He was a
caramel-colored brother with light hazel eyes. He was tall, at
least six-five, and very handsome – and from what I could tell,
he probably had a pretty nice body under his blue Gap shirt
and leather jacket.

"Hey," Alana said cheerily. "This is my friend Mark. We
went to college together."

"You went to Howard?" I asked nervously, thinking he
could possibly know Todd.

"Well, I actually went to UCLA before transferring to
Howard," Alana answered for him, clearing up my confusion.

"Oh, I see," I said as I breathed a soft sigh of relief.

"Mark, this is my girl Kai," Alana said.

I extended my hand to him as we locked eyes, and a broad
smile crawled across his face. The brother was not only handsome – he had great teeth, too.

"So were you guys in the same year?" I said.

"No, actually, I was four years ahead of Alana," Mark said.

"And he never gave me the time of day that first year,
which is why I left," Alana said jokingly.

"Are you kidding me? You just don't remember. Not to
mention you were one of the hottest freshman to hit the campus that year," Mark said with a flirtatious twang in his voice.
Alana blushed as she looked at me, then back at Mark.

This made me sit up and pay attention as I saw that they
kind of liked each other.

"So can I buy you guys a drink?" Mark asked.

Alana looked at me, and she knew I was so ready to leave.
Not to mention three was starting to feel a bit, well, crowded in
our bed/booth.

"Actually, Mark, we're about to get out of here, but maybe we can continue this conversation at a later date?" Alana said assertively.

"No doubt," Mark responded as he pulled out a business card and handed it to Alana.

"Thanks, I'll call you," Alana said.

"Cool, I look forward to it," Mark replied, "and it was nice meeting you, Kai."

"Likewise."

"Have a good night," Alana said as she played with Mark's card.

"You, too," Mark said as he flashed his million-dollar smile then turned and walked away.

"Damn, I can't believe I ran into Mark Elliott," Alana said. "He was so damn fine in college and, well, he still is."

"So you like him?" I asked.

"Hell, yeah, kinda hard not to, the brother is fiiiine!" Alana exclaimed.

I was starting to feel a sense of jealously that I shouldn't have felt, but I couldn't hide my feelings. How could I justify being jealous of Alana liking another guy when I had a man sitting at home? I told myself to brush it off and keep it moving.

As we headed out of Blu, Alana needed to stop at the bathroom so I patiently waited outside. As I leaned against the cold cement wall I glanced over to my left to see Mark staring back at me. He gave me a look that I couldn't quite decipher as I turned away to look down at my black Prada strap-backs with the maroon tips. One thing I loved was a great shoe, if nothing else. I would spend my whole month's salary on them if I didn't have other responsibilities like rent, food, and, yes, coffee.

I looked back up to see that Mark was gone. I wondered what was taking Alana so long, so I tapped on the bathroom door, then turned the knob. The door swung open. I guess Alana figured she didn't need to lock it since I was outside standing guard. As I entered I caught Alana's reflection in the mirror as she was stroking on a fresh coat of lip-gloss. Her eyes were a bit red from the three drinks she'd had that night, and we both were very tipsy. I shut the door behind me, locking it. Alana turned to me, giving me a look.

"You gotta go?" Alana asked, now primping in the mirror as if she was getting ready to go out rather than go home.

I shook my head and walked over to her. I don't know what was coming over me but I needed to kiss her. I stopped in front of her, looking deep in her eyes, but not really knowing what I wanted to say,; maybe because it wasn't words I wanted to share with her. I rubbed her stomach from behind as I moved my hand up towards her breast. Alana looked down at my hand and up at the mirror returning my stare in our reflections.

"What are you doing, Kai?"

"What do you think?" I responded.

"I think you're trying to seduce me, that's what, in a public restroom, I might add."

"Maybe," I said as I turned her around towards me, leaning my body against hers as I slowly went in for a kiss, which turned into a longer kiss, which turned into us kissing and grinding against the wall. I reached to unbuckle Alana's jeans when a knock at the door scared the hell out of us. We both jumped way too suddenly, then laughed at what we were attempting to do. The knock got louder and more intense.

"We're coming!" Alana yelled back as she adjusted her clothes and re-applied her lipstick.

"We'd better go," I said.

"Rain check?" Alana asked as she glided her fingers across my right nipple, sending a pleasant sensation through my body, before heading for the door.

We left Blu and headed home, but I was silent as Alana picked up where she left off about Mark. She was definitely high on this guy and the more she spoke of him the more frustrated I got, but I sat there and just let her talk, since there was nothing I could say without sounding completely nuts.

Alana pulled up in front of my house and we shared a silent moment before she said, "I had fun with you tonight, Kai."

"Me, too," I said with a convincing tone. Although my good time ended when Mark stepped into the picture, I decided to just keep that to myself.

I started to get out of the car when I felt Alana touch my arm. "I can't have a kiss goodnight?" she asked.

I closed the door, took a quick look outside, just to make sure the coast was clear before leaning in to give Alana a quick peck on the lips. I opened the door again, then felt Alana grab my hand – again.

"Kai?"

"Yeah?"

"I also liked how aggressive you were tonight," Alana said. "It turned me on."

"Really?"

"Yeah."

I smiled, knowing that my aggressiveness stemmed from pure jealously of her old college acquaintance who had interrupted our night of solitude – but like I said, who was I to be jealous? I jumped out the car and headed into my house to be with Todd.

24 · HIDDEN SECRETS

YOU WOULD HAVE THOUGHT Oprah herself was coming to dinner the way my mom was acting. When you haven't had a boyfriend in a while, the moment you finally get one is a monumental event in the Edwards home.

Todd and I jumped into a cab and headed to my mother's dinner party. I always liked to cab it when I went to one of her parties, because the one thing that got me through the night was an excess amount of alcohol. And I usually didn't plan on being in any condition to drive afterwards.

I was quiet, thinking about how jealous I became when Alana brought her new friend over to meet me. I hated that feeling, especially when it was with someone I shouldn't even be with. My cell phone rang and I looked at it; it was Alana. I hit "Ignore," sending her into voicemail. Two seconds later Todd's phone rang, but unlike me, he answered his. And no surprise – it was Alana.

"Hey!" Todd sang into the phone.

I looked over at Todd as his whole demeanor changed. I just shook my head and looked away. But just as quickly as I looked away, I snapped my head back when I heard, coming out of Todd's mouth, "We're headed to Kai's parents for a dinner party, you want to come?"

I gave Todd a look of death. What the hell was he doing?

"Oh, hold on, let me see if it is okay with Kai," Todd said as he pulled the phone away from his ear. I was sure he saw the steam rising from my neck.

If murder were legal I would have stabbed Todd in his neck with my three-inch Jimmy Choo spiked heel. How dare he put me on the spot! If I said "No," I'd look like the bitch.

I turned to Todd with a slight smile. "I'm sure my mom won't mind," I said through gritted teeth.

Todd hung up the phone and I turned to him. "What the hell is wrong with you?"

"What?"

"Just inviting Alana like that, not to mention, putting me on the spot. I didn't ask my mom if I could bring anyone extra."

"Kai," Todd said, "you're always saying how your mom loves tons of people at her parties. Now there will just be more to envy her."

I turned away and rolled my eyes; the last thing I wanted was my mother to meet my boyfriend for the first time not to mention the woman that I am fucking. How more perfect could that be.

"Baby, I'm sorry, I can call her and tell her not to come."

"Yeah, and make me look like the wicked bitch of the Midwest, no thank you."

"I can just tell her…" Todd said, his voice trailing off.

"Forget it Todd, don't worry about it, really."

"Sorry, I just thought it would be cool."

I turned my head and we rode the rest of the way in silence. We arrived in front of my mom's house just as Alana was walking up.

Alana and I locked eyes as she and Todd gave each other a friendly hug.

"Hey," I said.

"Hey, Kai, did you forget your phone at home?"

I knew what Alana was doing, throwing it out there that she, indeed, had called me and I, indeed, had not answered.

"No, I um, must have it on vibrate."

"Right," Alana said without trying to sound convincing.

As we walked towards the door in silence, I was very nervous about Alana coming with us to my parent's house – but what the hell, there was no turning back now. I would just pass her off as Todd best friend. I mean, no one had to know that I was sleeping with her, too.

"Darling!" my mother sang as she swung open the front door to reveal me, Todd, and Alana, the happy threesome.

"Hey, Corrine," I said with a smile.

"Todd," my mom said, "it is so nice to finally meet you. I was starting to think that Kai was making you up. Then again she did have a vivid imagination as a child – did she ever tell you about her ten-inch bedside friends that would keep her company when she would sleep on her own?"

"Mom, we don't need to bore Todd with childhood stories," I said, quickly cutting off "Chatty Kathy" before Todd did a beeline out of the house and out of my life. Todd extended his hand.

"Well, it is nice to finally meet you, Mrs. Edwards," Todd said, smiling from ear to ear.

"Are you kidding me?" my mom exclaimed, "you better give me a hug. It's not too often that Kai brings home a decent man these days. And by all means, please call me Corrine, I mean my own children do, so why not you too?" My mom glanced over at me then turned her attention to Alana.

"And who might you be?" Corrine continued, this time with more of an interrogating tone.

"Oh, this is Alana, Todd's best friend," I said, making sure the "best friend" was emphasized.

"Well, it is nice to meet you Alana. What a pretty girl you are."

"Thank you," Alana said with a smile.

"Actually, Alana is also one of the models for my 'Just B' campaign," I added.

"Just what, honey?" Corrine asked, her face turning up to one side.

"The campaign Simone and I are working on with singer/songwriter Bianca."

Corinne held her quizzical look. Classic Corrine – she only remembered things beneficial to her.

"Actually, the campaign is pretty amazing, I love the different slogans: Just B sexy, Just B positive, Just B love," Alana said, trying to jog Corrine's memory.

"Of course, right, now I remember, that's great honey. I know it will be a huge success since you are working on it," Corinne said.

I hated how I always had to jog Corrine's memory every time something about my work came up, but then again, I am talking about my mother, Miss Self-Absorbed. I love her but she really did live for the woman looking back at her from that vanity mirror.

"Well, enough of the small talk, come, come, in we go, there are already a few guests here," Corinne said as she herded us in the house.

We all trailed in the house following my mother like goslings following their mother goose. We entered the dining room to see the table set for ten. I looked around, wondering who else would be here that night, and then I heard the doorbell ring.

"That should be Mila and Charles," Corrine said as she disappeared down the hall to collect yet two more guests for her oh-so-grand dinner party.

Todd, Alana, and I just stood there, not really knowing what to do or where to turn. I felt just as awkward as they did, and in my own parent's home. I needed a drink.

"So, does anyone want a drink?" I asked, directing my question to Todd and Alana.

"Yeah, sure," they said in unison.

"Be right back," I said as I headed towards the kitchen to grab three glasses and a bottle of pinot griot. As I began to open the bottle, I had to stop and think; I mean, just in the next room were Todd - my boyfriend, and Alana - my, well, the woman that I am currently sleeping with. For some odd reason the thought brought a smile to my face.

I turned to see Mila standing in the doorway. I jumped a bit, not expecting anyone to be there. "Hey, you scared me!"

"Why is that, Kai? Were you doing something you weren't supposed to be doing?" Mila asked as she entered the kitchen.

"No, Mila." I said rolling my eyes. Ever since we were kids, Mila's mission was to catch me doing something wrong. She really needed to get a life.

"So, I just met your new boyfriend. Very handsome, I have to say. Is this one for keeps or just another ship passing in the night?" Mila asked with a sarcastic smirk on her face. My sister had a way of getting her digs in, any way she could.

"Well, I hope so, and for your good, Mila. I'm sure you're getting tired of coming up with all those witty comments."

Mila ignored my comeback as she walked over to the counter and poured herself a glass of wine. "So who's the girl on his arm?"

"Excuse me?" I asked.

"The arm piece."

"First of all, she is not on Todd's arm, and secondly, she is his best friend."

Mila took a sip of her wine. "Pretty nice looking best

friend, if you ask me."

"How about I don't ask you, then?"

"Well, you should," Mila said.

"Mila, what is your problem?"

Mila set down her wine glass and turned to me. "Oh, I don't have a problem, but you may."

"Okay, what are you getting at?" I asked.

"Just be careful who your man calls his best friend, that's all."

"Yeah, I'll be sure to take that advice, especially since it's coming from you," I said, hoping she'd catch the oozing sarcasm in my voice.

"If you're smart you'd take that advice from anybody," Mila said as she poured herself a little more wine from the bottle, and then picked up her glass again. "You don't want to wake up and have your man leaving you for his so-called 'best friend.'"

"I'm pretty sure that won't happen, Mila," I said, thinking if Mila only knew.

"Hmm, famous last words," Mila replied. "I say, don't let them come back and bite you in the ass, Kai."

"Whatever Mila."

"Don't say you haven't been warned," she said,

I ignored Mila as I watched her head out of the kitchen. I took a deep breath and went out myself. I walked over to where Todd and Alana were standing. Corrine and Mila were chatting them both up, or should I say getting as much info to use against me as possible.

As the night progressed, I had to take a break and retreat to my old bedroom, now a guest room-slash-den. I sat on the day bed, taking in the memories of the days I'd spent in this house. I had to work hard to block out the many bad memories and think hard to remember the good ones. I looked up to see Alana standing in the doorway.

"How long have you been standing there?" I asked.

"Not long."

Alana entered the room and sat next to me on the bed.

"You okay?" Alana asked.

"I'm good, just taking in the night," I said. "My family can be a bit much, as you can tell."

"Yeah, but I'm sure they mean well."

"Or at least they act like it," I said.

I looked at Alana and couldn't believe how attracted I was to her. I loved how she looked at me when she spoke. When I looked at her I was able to see myself in a much deeper and fuller way now.

"Hey, so sorry for crashing your mother's dinner party."

"Really?"

"No," Alana said. "But I wanted to see you and, well, I knew you would keep blowing me off."

"Alana, I'm not blowing you off, I'm just being careful. And you inviting yourself and putting me, you, and Todd in the same room, is not being careful."

"Well, as long as we don't make it obvious, then he has nothing to find out."

"Please," I said, "you are over-the-top obvious sometimes."

"Not always, I just like being around you, Kai."

Alana and I stared quietly at one another for a moment. "I like being around you, too," I said.

I took a deep breath, and thought of Todd and what he would do if he found out.

"So, do you think Todd suspects anything?" I asked.

"I doubt it. If you haven't already noticed, your man is pretty absorbed in his practice right now."

"This is true. But what if he did figure something out, do you think he would say something?"

"Kai, stop worrying, okay?" Alana replied.

"I know, but it's hard. And you can't blame me for feeling weird."

"I understand," she said, "but don't let it mess up what we

have."

Alana put her hand on my leg. She leaned in and kissed me gently on the lips; I kissed her back, then quickly realized where we were and what we were doing. I pulled back.

"Alana," I said, "we can't do this here. This is what I'm talking about – Todd is right downstairs. What if he comes upstairs?"

Alana sat back, crossing her arms. "Kai, I told him I was going to check on you so he thinks we're just talking. Where's your sense of adventure?" Alana leaned back in and began to kiss me again, this time on my cheek, then making her way to my neck, then closing in on my lips. I gave in and we fell back onto the bed. Alana crawled on top of me as we kissed and caressed each other. I started to lose myself in her when I heard a thump. I jumped up.

"What was that?" I asked.

"What was what?" Alana murmured as she continued to kiss me.

"That noise, did you hear it? Like a thump," I said as I pushed Alana off me and sat up.

"No, Kai, you're just being paranoid," Alana insisted.

"Paranoid or not, we shouldn't be doing this in my parents' house," I said as I started fixing my clothes and hair.

"Fine," Alana said with a bit of irritation in her voice. I chose to ignore it because Alana didn't have as much to lose as I did if someone had happened to see us.

"Come on, let's go back downstairs," I said as I stood up and adjusted my clothes.

"Fine, Kai, let's go," Alana agreed.

As Alana and I headed back downstairs to rejoin the dinner party, I wondered if that thump I'd heard really was just a figment of my imagination.

25 · A SHARED MOMENT

TODD SLEPT AS I watched him. I looked at his peaceful face and felt a sense of comfort within me. It had been close to eight months since Todd and I started dating and I couldn't see being with any other man. I knew that I could marry him and I hoped he felt the same.

Todd woke to me staring down at him. He smiled as he reached out to me.

"What are you doing?" Todd asked in his sleepy voice as he stretched his long muscular body.

"Just watching you sleep," I said as I stroked his warm face. Todd reached out and pulled me in close to him, spooning me from behind. His warm, hard body felt good against mine and I felt his manhood growing.

"I love you, you know that?" Todd whispered in my ear.

"I love you, too," I said.

"Do you really?" Todd asked with a concerned tone.

"Of course I do, why are you saying it like that?" I asked as I turned to look in his eyes.

"I don't know, it just seems lately you've been kinda distant."

"Distant how?"

"Your mind seems like it is somewhere else that's all. I just want to make sure that you're still happy," he said.

I turned my body completely toward Todd as he sat up.

"So, are you still happy?" Todd asked.

"Yes, baby, I am."

"And you still want to be with me?"

"Of course I do," I said.

"So there's, you know, no other guy?"

A shiver of fear rushed through my body. I sat up and faced Todd. He waited patiently for an answer. Todd looked like a child, innocence and eagerness all wrapped up in one.

"No, there's no other man," I answered. "You are the only man in my life."

A broad smile crawled across Todd's face as well as a flash of confidence.

"Well, you can't blame a brother for checking," Todd said. "We have to do that sometimes, y'know?"

"Yeah, I'm sure – you and that ego of yours," I said in a playful tone. I leaned in and gave Todd a kiss on the lips. "So let me ask you a question."

"Okay," he said.

"Would you break up with me if I cheated on you?"

Todd was silent; he looked deep in my eyes, and then away, then back again.

"But you haven't, right?"

"No, but what if I did, would you break up with me?" I asked again.

Todd was silent again. He took a deep breath, continued to think, then, "Yea, I think I would. It would be hard, but I would."

Then I said something that surprised even myself, something I knew I had to get out, but couldn't say directly.

"What if I cheated with a girl?"

"A girl?" Todd repeated.

"Yeah."

I knew I was skating on thin ice, but it was too late to turn back; I was already in the middle of the pond. I held my breath, waiting for what Todd would say.

"No."

"Why?" I said as I silently breathed a sigh of relief.

"Because it's a girl, and to me, that doesn't seem like cheating."

'Why not?" I asked.

"I don't know," Todd said. "It's just different. I mean, you're just licking her and she's just licking you, which is kind of hot."

Todd raised his eyebrow and cocked his head to the side.

"Why are you asking me this, are you thinking about getting with a girl?"

"I think every woman thinks about it once or twice in her life, but not all women act on it," I said.

"So would you?" he asked.

"Would I what?"

"Act on it, you know, get with a girl?"

I paused, thinking this could be my "in," the way I could eventually break the news that I was sleeping with Alana. But something was stopping me, something I couldn't explain.

"No."

"Well if you wanted to," Todd continued, "I'd be down with that. I mean, two times the fun, right?"

I laughed but it was more of a laugh of relief than anything, but I also was a was a little taken aback at my man's eagerness to get it on with two women. But in that moment I thought about what Simone had said, how every man loved the idea until it became reality.

"Why does every man have that fantasy?" I asked.

"Because it's hot, two women together."

"What about two men?" I said.

"Not so hot," Todd quickly said.

"Now wait a minute, Denzel Washington plus The Rock isn't a bad thought."

"No baby, that's just wrong in so many ways," Todd said.

"Well, it depends on who you ask."

"Is that right?" Todd asked as he grabbed me and playfully threw me down on the bed. We began to kiss passionately, and then he pulled away.

"I'm very happy right now."

"You are?" I asked.

"Yes, because I have a growing practice, a great home, and a beautiful girlfriend," Todd said as he kissed on my neck. "I don't think a man could be any happier right now."

As Todd kissed every inch of my body I wondered if I had missed my opportunity to come clean and tell Todd the truth, knowing then where he stood about my being with a woman. But then I thought about it a little more and decided that my being with just any woman was different than my being with a woman he called his best friend. That is where the hurt and the deceit were, being so close to home. I closed my eyes and tried to focus completely in taking in all of Todd's affection, but I still couldn't shake the guilt that came with sleeping with Alana, my man's best friend.

26 · RAYMOND RETURNS

"Hey sis!" Raymond's voice startled me as I looked up from my mailbox to find him standing in the lobby of my condo.

Urine with a healthy dash of seven day body odor was my brother's fragrance of choice. He stood a mere ten feet away from me, but I could smell his stench as if we were engaged in a full embrace. I slowly closed my mailbox and turned towards him.

"Raymond, where have you been?" I asked, noticing his frail body and gaunt face, more so than usual. It was apparent that my brother had finally hit rock bottom, which brought him directly to my doorstep.

"I've been around, you know, taking care of business, you know," he said in a nervous chatter, and avoiding direct eye contact.

"You can't just disappear like that," I said. "It's been two months, and I didn't know if you were dead or alive."

"I know and I'm sorry," Raymond said, as he twitched and smiffled. "I'm also sorry about that situation back at the hospital, stickin' you with the bill and all. I'll pay you back, I promise, right when I get me another job. Actually, I got this job lined up, and I'll know something in a few days, or weeks, I think."

As Raymond spoke, I observed him almost involuntarily shifting his weight back and forth and from side to side with erratic movements. Unaware to himself that he was doing it. This was Raymond's way of pacifying himself.

"Don't worry about the money, Raymond, it's no big deal, really," I said, knowing it was a big fucking deal, but getting three thousand back from Raymond wasn't going to happen anytime soon, or should I say, not in this lifetime.

"Thanks, sis, I, I owe you one. Listen, you mind if I come up, to, uh, talk, I really need to talk, sis," Raymond said.

It was an awkward moment. I didn't feel comfortable inviting Raymond into my home, but at the same time, I didn't want anyone to see me with him in my lobby. I threw my keys back in my purse along with my few envelopes of mail.

"Let's take a walk," I said, heading toward him.

Raymond and I walked the streets until we found an empty park bench. I could tell that my brother was a little different than normal. His eyes showed helplessness, desperation and self-pity.

Raymond and I sat in silence for a few minutes without saying a word to each other. I really didn't have anything to say; I mean, I'd run out of things to say to someone who merely existed, taking what he could get and moving on. I felt for a minute that Raymond was out of words himself, but then he surprised me.

"I wanna go to rehab, sis," Raymond said as he looked at me then quickly back down to the ground.

Raymond rubbed his hands together as if he were massaging lotion into his palms. His leg was bouncing up and down and I could tell that he had nowhere else to go.

"Are you sure about this?"

Raymond looked up at me. "I am."

"Where? I mean, back to the same place?"

"No, there's this church on 55th and State, they have a good rehab center, supposed to get you clean."

Raymond looked up at me with a glimmer of hope in his eyes. "Sis, I wanna get clean, for real this time."

Raymond has wanted to get clean for ten years now, but this time felt different. Still, I had to make sure of it.

"After four attempts, how is this one different?" I asked, hoping to hear a new answer.

Raymond dropped his head in his hands and began rubbing his fingers through his matted hair, almost like he was giving himself a head massage. He finally looked back up at me with tears in his eyes.

"I can't live like this anymore, it's not supposed to be like this, sis," Raymond said as he wiped the tears from his eyes. The dirt from his fingers left grey and black streaks across his face.

"I'm sick and I need help, and if I can't get help I just don't know if I can live another day like this."

"Raymond, don't say that, don't ever say that. Nothing in life should make you want to end yours," I said, almost begging my brother to get that tragic thought out of his head.

"I'm sorry, sis, but I can't help how I feel. I just can't."

I reached out and pulled Raymond to me, ignoring the smell and the way that he looked and just embraced the man that I called my brother.

For the first time, I saw the years of pain escaping my brothers limp, fragile body. I held back my tears, trying to think of how I could help Raymond, help him escape from the demons that had taken over his body, taken over his mind. At times I wondered how it felt to have a substance control your every desire, your every whim, your every waking moment. But in a sense, I was living the same life, minus the needle sticking out of my arm and the glass pipe in my mouth. My addiction came in the form of a woman, Alana, she was draining my life out of me, making it hard for me to get through the day, to think clearly, and sometimes even to eat. In a sense I needed some kind of rehab just as much as my brother did, but I was in denial, not truly believing that something was in control of my life. I didn't want to face the reality that Alana had a hold on me.

"How much does it cost, the rehab center?" I asked.

Raymond looked down, then back up, wiping off the snot that was running from his nose.

"Five thousand dollars."

I took a deep breath, I didn't have five thousand dollars, let alone the three thousand I paid for his hospital visit.

"That's a lot of money," I said.

"I know, sis, I know."

I felt sick, because I knew I was his only hope and I knew I couldn't afford it. "I don't have five thousand dollars, Raymond. I wish I did, but I don't."

Raymond dropped his head back into his hands, "Maybe you could ask Mila for it, her husband is rich, they have it, and you can tell her it's for you, an emergency or something. I really need to do this and I don't see any other way, sis."

I looked Raymond in his eyes and for the first time he did not break our stare before saying, "I don't know if I can make it through another day."

"Raymond, please stop saying that," I pleaded.

"Sorry, sis, I just feel so lost," Raymond said.

I thought about my parents, and how they had vowed never to spend another dime on Raymond after he single-handedly drained them of nearly forty thousand dollars, and then stomped on their hearts as well as their pride. I knew that my parents were out of the question, but Mila – I might be able to sway her. Maybe.

I took a deep breath, and had to think hard about what I was going to say, think about the ramifications and possible consequences of my next words. "Let me see what I can do with Mila."

A few more tears fell from my brother's eyes, tears of hope, hope that his days of living that wretched life would soon be behind him.

"Thanks, sis."

"It's all right, Raymond, it's all right.

27 · JUDGEMENT DAY

I DECIDED TO HEAD over to Mila's house since she had not returned any of my phone calls for a few days. It had been a week since Raymond mentioned that he wanted to go to rehab and I needed to feel Mila out about pitching in.

I thought about asking Todd, but I knew his money was tied up in his new practice. And besides, this was my problem, not his, and I didn't want him to think that he needed to help bail out my brother.

I jumped on Lakeshore Drive and headed south towards Hyde Park, exited on 53rd street, headed west to Kenwood Avenue, and arrived in front of Mila's two-story, upper-middle class home. I rang the doorbell and waited patiently for a response. I was just about to turn and walk away when one of the double doors swung open and Mila stood there with a half smile, half "what are you doing here?" look on her face. Mila looked half asleep, although she probably was wide awake but just didn't have any makeup on. She was sporting a pink velvet sweatsuit with matching fluffy slippers. She glanced at her watch.

"What are you doing here?"

"Well," I replied, "since you haven't been returning my calls I had to stop by. There is something I need to talk to you about."

Mila just stood there as if wondering about letting me in. I couldn't figure out what her issue was, but honestly, I didn't have the time or patience to figure it out.

"Can I come in?" I asked with a slightly annoyed ring in my voice.

"Yeah, but just for a minute, I just put the twins down."

I followed Mila into her house. The air in the room was filled with a strange scent; I couldn't tell if it was cheap or expensive perfume, but it smelled like it was mixed with a store brand air spray. Mila headed to the kitchen, sat down at the table, and continued to polish her silverware, something I obviously interrupted with my unannounced visit.

I sat down next to her at the kitchen table. Mila acted as if I wasn't even there.

"So listen, Mila, Raymond came to see me last week," I said.

Mila stopped for a moment upon hearing our brother's name, but then quickly went back to her polishing. I knew our brother's name would cause a ripple in the rigid flow of her life, but I also knew she would pretend it didn't bother her.

"He's not doing too well," I said.

"So what else is new," Mila stated with a cold, harsh tone.

"Mila, can you muster up a little compassion?" I asked. "He is your brother, for Christ's sake."

"What do you want me to say, Kai?" Mila asked.

"Hell, I don't know," I replied. "Maybe 'how is he,' 'where is he,' 'is he dead,' 'is he alive,' 'did he OD?'"

"Well, did he?" Mila asked.

"Did he what, Mila?"

"Did he OD?"

"Unbelievable," I said. "No Mila, he didn't. He wants to go to rehab"

"Again?"

"Yes, again."

"Well, I'm not giving him a dime," Mila said as she went back to her polishing.

"Why am I not surprised."

"Save it, Kai, okay? As far as I'm concerned you wasted a trip over here, because I would rather eat glass then give Raymond any of my money."

"You mean your husband's money," I shot back.

I hated to have to go there, but Mila's holier-than-thou disposition was pissing me off and I wanted to check her real quickly.

Mila gave me a look of death, a look I had never seen before.

"It's our money, and Raymond's not getting any of it. Matter of fact, you can leave now."

"What the hell is your problem, Mila? What did I do to deserve your infamous shitty attitude?"

Mila didn't answer, and I was not in the mood to play her stupid guessing games.

"Fine, I'm outta here," I said. "You have a great heart, you know that? I'm sure you'll go far with that." I stood to leave when Mila said something that paralyzed my next step.

"I saw you kissing her."

A cold shiver shot through my body, as if I'd stepped out naked into a frigid Chicago winter day.

I slowly turned back toward my sister, who was leaning back in her seat with her arms folded ever so tightly across her chest, a look of grave disapproval plastered on her face.

"What did you say?" I asked, making sure I had heard her

correctly, making sure my anger towards her hadn't distorted the words that were coming out of her mouth.

"I saw you kissing Todd's best friend, what's her name? Alana is it?"

My mind began to work overtime, trying to figure out exactly when Mila could have seen Alana and me. I thought I had been extra careful, but I guess I hadn't been careful enough. Maybe Mila was bluffing – how could she have known?

"The next time you wanna make out with your little girl-friend in our parents' house, you may want to shut the bed-room door first."

In that moment I was brought back to the scene of the crime, the night of my mother's dinner party, when Alana kissed me as we sat on my bed. That noise I'd heard, that thump, it had not been my imagination. It was Mila. Fuck me.

I stood there for a minute trying to think of ways to spin it, hoping I could make Mila believe that she really didn't see what she thought she saw, but as I saw her glaring back at me I knew that there was no spinning this one, not in my wildest dreams. So I threw out an "I don't give a fuck" response. "Well, so what."

Mila chuckled, unfolded her arms, and carefully folded her hands on the table as if about to say a prayer. "Is that all you have to say – 'So what?'"

I was getting madder by the second, and hated how conde-scending and judgmental Mila could be. And she was in rare form.

"What do you want me to say, Mila? So what, I kissed her, it's not a big deal," I said, trying to minimize the whole situa-tion, trying to make my most embarrassing moment not feel so devastating.

"Did you fuck her, too?" Mila asked with a smirk.

"That's none of your business. Matter of fact, this whole situation is none of your damn business, Mila."

"If you ask me," she said, "this whole girl-on-girl phenomenon is fucking disgusting."

"Well, how about I don't ask you then, okay? How about you take your judgmental and uptight ass and go to hell?"

I started to feel nauseous as I tried desperately to stay strong, to keep my composure. I felt completely exposed, as my sister began seeing me in a totally different light, a light that revealed things she considered despicable.

I turned to leave, not wanting to finish the conversation, feeling embarrassed and exposed, feeling like an open wound. I headed to the door.

"So, what, are you a lesbian now?" Mila called out as she stood and began to walk behind me. I turned to look at her.

"Screw you, Mila," I shot back.

"I guess that explains why you never had a 'real' boyfriend. All makes sense now."

I stopped, turning to face my evil twin. "Mila, you know why I never had a boyfriend."

Mila chuckled. "Oh, right, 'the dreams,'" Mila said in a sarcastic tone as she made air quotes with her fingers.

"They weren't just dreams," I said.

"Of course, they really happened. You know, Kai, you were always so great at telling stories, and I often wondered if what you claimed happened, really happened."

"You know it did," I said.

"I have to say, I do have doubts. I mean, we all have our doubts," Mila said.

I'm not a violent person, but in that moment I wanted to hurt my twin sister, make her feel the pain that she had forever denied that I felt. Simply put, I wanted to knock her fucking block off.

But instead, I headed towards the door, but not before hearing Mila's last words.

"Don't worry, I won't tell your boyfriend. I'm sure fucking his best friend will eventually rear its ugly head on its own."

Mila walked around me, then stopped. "And just think, I would have put my money on Todd fucking Alana. Who knew it would have been you?" Mila chuckled.

I fought back the tears as I headed out her house, feeling numb, pissed, and nauseous all at once. What if Mila did tell Todd, how would I explain it? Although I knew that Alana and I had a pact not to tell, Mila didn't have anything to lose, not a goddamn thing. I headed to my car but could not hold back my tears. I jumped in and before I even closed the door I broke down.

I cried for twenty minutes before I was able to drive away.

28 · A FRIEND IN NEED

I FOUND MYSELF KNOCKING on Simone's door at 9:30pm. I had sat in my car in front of her house for two hours before finally deciding to go in. I didn't want to go home and face Todd, I wasn't strong enough, I needed to talk to a friend who wouldn't pass judgment on me, and that's why I headed to Simone's house.

Simone opened the door. I must've looked like hell.

"What happened?" Simone gasped.

I opened my mouth to tell her about my encounter with Mila, but all I could manage was a high-pitched cry.

In short order, I told Simone everything that had transpired with Mila. I was able to discuss the embarrassment and shame I carried away from the horrific situation. For the first time I felt weird about having been with a woman. Mila had made me feel dirty and sinful, as if I had done something for which I should be executed for.

"I know that's your twin sister, but she is a first-class bitch. How did you turn out so normal and she, well, could double for Satan."

"I am certainly not normal," I said. "As far as Mila, she's just unhappy, been that way since she got married. That's what happens when you marry for money."

"Take it from me," Simone replied. "I didn't marry for money, hell, I didn't even marry for love. I married for sex."

"Sex?"

"That's right," Simone said. "The night I realized my husband could eat my pussy and fuck me just as well, was the night I knew he was the one."

We had a good laugh with that one. I loved how Simone could brighten any dark moment with a flip of her tongue.

"But on the real, Kai, don't let Mila steal your energy, it's not worth it. And whatever you do, don't let her make you think that sleeping with a woman is wrong, because it's not."

I took a deep breath as I lay back on Simone's off-white slipcover chaise. I loved her condo; it was so inviting and comfortable, I could have stayed there for days and just disappeared.

Simone sat across from me on her matching couch, sipping on her tea.

"Do you think she'll tell Todd?" I asked.

"Well, she is evil, but she is still your sister and deep down, under that bitter shell of hatred, she does love you. Besides, I think she would rather keep you wondering than just put it out there."

"That's certainly true," I agreed.

"Listen sweetie," Simone said. "What you're doing is, well, different, but clearly you have feelings or Alana. My advice? Be careful, especially if you want to keep Todd in your life."

I thought about what Simone said. People have affairs everyday, but to cheat with your man's best friend, who's a woman, is definitely different.

"What would you do? I asked her.

"Honestly, I would do what made me happy. If it's being with Alana, then come clean with Todd, and vice versa. But I think seeing both of them will only end badly."

"I want to keep Todd," I said. "I don't know what I would do if I lost him."

"It sounds like you've already made up your mind."

"Yeah, I guess I have," I sighed. "I need to end my affair with Alana."

"So when are you going to do it?"

"Soon," I said, feeling safe in Simone's living room, in my own personal retreat.

I needed to find the strength to end the double life I was living, before anyone else found out and it got back to Todd.

29 · TRUTH BE TOLD

I ASKED ALANA TO meet me for a drink. I had decided to break it off with her. I needed to go through with it before I lost the nerve. I was nervous because I was still very attracted to Alana, and that was just part of her hold over me.

In that moment I thought about my brother and how his addiction was taking over his life, but how he was taking steps to fix it, to free himself of it. His drug of choice was cocaine, while mine was Alana. I needed to follow in his footsteps, take action to fix this wrong I had created in my life, end it once and for all before my addiction took over and ruined everything I had ever hoped for and dreamed of. I had to end it before it ended me.

I arrived at the Table 6 restaurant on Ontario Street around 8:15pm and headed for the bar. I ordered a shot of tequila, quickly followed that up with a glass of wine. Alana arrived twenty minutes later. At first glance told me she was in a good mood.

"Hey, honey," Alana said as she took the seat next to me at the bar. She gave me a friendly rub on the leg before waving down the bartender. "So what's up? I was excited to get your call. I was missing you."

I smiled at Alana as I drank down the rest of my wine.

"Listen, Alana, I –"

"Hey," Alana said, cutting me off, "you wanna check out this new lounge? It's just down the street from here and I heard it was pretty nice." Alana had a lot of energy and I wasn't sure where it was coming from.

"Actually, Alana, I'm kinda tired."

"Are you okay?" Alana asked as she grabbed her drink and took a few sips from it.

"I'm fine," I replied. "I'm just not in the lounge mood, ya know?"

"No worries, maybe another time," Alana said as her cell phone went off. She glanced at the display. "I gotta get this, it's Mark," Alana said as she flipped open her phone. "Hey, baby. I'm having drinks with Kai." She paused, then giggled into the receiver.

I turned away, feeling a little like a jealous third wheel. I kept telling myself that my feelings for Alana would subside after a while but it was a slow road.

Alana finished up her conversation and hung up. "Sorry about that," she said as she lightly caressed my leg.

"So how are you and Mark doing?" I asked.

"We're cool."

"So are you guys a couple now?"

"I guess you could say that," Alana sheepishly smiled like a schoolgirl with a new love interest.

I really didn't know why I was even inquiring about Alana's personal life, seeing that my main goal of meeting her was not to get a run down on who she was fucking but to break it off with her, once and for all. So I took another sip of my drink and told myself to stay focused.

"So Alana, I wanted to talk to you about something."

"I wanted to talk to you about something as well," Alana said, totally cutting me off again. "Tomorrow is Mark's birthday and I want to get him something special."

"Um okay," I mumbled.

"So I was thinking that maybe we could fulfill one of his fantasies," Alana said, giving me a seductive look.

"Which is?" I wondered aloud.

Alana took a sip of her drink and swiveled her bar stool to face me. "Being with two women, of course."

"What man doesn't have that fantasy?" I asked as I flagged the bartender down for another drink.

"So how about it?" Alana asked with a huge grin on her face.

I looked back at her. "How about what?" I inquired.

"How about having a threesome with us?"

"Are you crazy?"

"It would be fun, and besides, I never wanted to do one of those until I met you," Alana replied. "I have to feel comfortable with a person, ya know."

"Actually, Alana –"

"Come on Kai, I would do it for you," Alana pleaded.

"No," I said. "You wouldn't."

"Yes, I would," Alana replied.

"So, you would do it with me and Todd?"

"Well, no, not Todd," Alana said, "but def if you had a different boyfriend."

"Why not Todd?" I pressed her.

"Because I've known Todd too long and besides, he couldn't handle seeing us together," Alana continued. "Trust me, I know him like the back of my hand."

I couldn't believe Alana was trying to get me to do a threesome with her and Mark, but more than that, I couldn't believe

I wasn't shutting the idea down immediately.

"So what I suggest is we have a few more drinks here, then head over to Mark's," Alana said.

"Alana, did you tell him about us?" I asked.

"Yeah, but he is totally cool about it, he won't tell anyone, he thinks it's hot."

"Alana," I said quietly, "no one should know."

"So you're telling me you haven't told Simone?" Alana asked.

"She's my best friend."

"And Mark is my man." Alana leaned in, giving me a pleading look. "Come on baby, do it for me, please? You'd make me really, really happy, not to mention think of how much fun it would be."

Alana continued to plead and I continued to have mixed emotions, I knew I should be breaking up with her right now, but a big part of me felt the urge to want to be with her. I sat there quietly as I pondered Alana's proposition. Alana put her hand back on my leg, this time massaging it even harder, "Kai, this would mean so much to me."

I sat there silently staring at Alana. I studied her hair, her eyes, her nose, her beautiful lips. Yep, Alana still had a hold over me and I hated it.

"Fine, but I can't stay all night," I relented.

"Yeees! Mark is going to be soooo excited!"

"I'm sure."

Alana flagged down the bartender. "Let's have a few more drinks on me, then we can go. Mark is waiting for us."

As we finished our last round and headed out the bar all I could think about was how Mila might handle this tidbit of information. I tried hard to shove that thought out of my head. Equally as disconcerting, my conscience was reminding me that not only would I be cheating with a woman, but this time I would be adding a man to the mix. Why wasn't I strong enough to go home? Why was I doing this to the man I love?

Why? That single word rang loud in my head. Why?

Simple: Because Alana was my drug and I needed another fix.

•

Before arriving at Mark's, I pulled Alana to the side to let her know that I was not, under any circumstances, doing anything with Mark; she could touch me but not him. Alana agreed, and said that she preferred it that way since she wasn't ready to see anyone else touch me in her presence. We entered Mark's condo and it was the quintessential bachelor pad. A bit on the small side, it was spartanly but tastefully furnished. There were candles lit everywhere, filling the room with a soft luminescent glow and a light fresh scent.

Mark was even better looking than I recall from our bried first meeting. He wore baggy jeans and a white wife-beater tank top. His arms were lean and cut, almost as if he had just finished pumping iron minutes before Alana and I walked through the door.

I sat alone in the living room on the couch as Mark and Alana talked in the kitchen. I could hear faint whispering accompanied by laughter, then gaps of silence. I wanted to go, I didn't really want to be there – but I did want to be with Alana. I took a deep breath and promised myself that this was it, this was absolutely the last time I would be with her.

Alana and Mark entered the living room, Alana with a drink in hand, Mark carrying two. Alana sat next to me as Mark leaned over and handed me the drink from his right hand, then seated himself in a chair directly in front of us. Mark made himself comfortable as if he was settling in for his favorite movie, with Alana and myself as the main attraction. I looked at Alana and she shot me a quick wink. Alana then raised her glass, and said, "A toast to fun times."

Mark chuckled, I drank, and Alana began kissing my neck soft and slow, but it quickly turned into a bit much. She was all over me before I had a chance to finish my damn drink. Her overly aggressive attitude was turning me off.

I pulled away from her. "What are you doing?" I whispered to Alana.

"I'm making out with you, come on baby, just relax," Alana said as she started to unbutton my shirt, kissing my chest with each button she opened. I looked over to see Mark smiling as he took slow sips from his glass, studying us as if he were watching a two bit peep show. His bulge was apparent through his jeans as he stroked it gently, watching. Alana opened my shirt, fully revealing my bra. I was immediately. I was immediately thankful that I'd worn matching panties. As Alana began kissing my neck and chest, Mark and I continued to hold a stare as our mutual girlfriend caressed and kissed my chest and slowly guided herself upwards to my lips. The moment we began to kiss I abandoned all restraint and really started get into it. Alana was the best kisser and she always pulled me into the moment with her soft lips and sensual tongue. I closed my eyes and felt myself pushing Alana down onto the couch when she pulled back.

"Not yet baby," Alana whispered.

"Why not?" I asked.

Alana didn't answer me, but stood and walked over to Mark. I watched as she straddled him and they began to kiss passionately and slowly grind. I felt awkward, as if I didn't belong, as if I shouldn't be there. But I damn sure wasn't leaving, leaving her with him. I wasn't sure what to do, so I continued to watch and continued to feel out of place and a little jealous and left out.

I finally stood and walked over to where they were; Alana felt my presence and stopped kissing Mark. She reached out to me and pulled me down to her and we began to kiss, right on Mark's lap. I felt Mark's arms wrap around the two of us, bringing us all in together. Alana pulled away from me and started kissing Mark again, then without stopping pulled me close to them and before I knew it we were all in a three-way kiss. Alana was working both Mark and me as she spread herself between the two of us. A three-way kiss was definitely a first for me, but it wasn't bad.

Alana then stopped and stood, grabbed my hand and pulled me back over to the couch. She looked over at Mark and said, "Baby, just watch, I wanna give you a show, okay?"

Mark smiled as he stood, unbuckled his belt, and stepped out of his pants, then quickly pulled off his black Calvin Klein boxers. His manhood was hard and very large and stood straight out with just a slight curve.

Alana smiled at the sight of Mark's penis. "Isn't his dick beautiful?" Alana asked.

I looked and smiled but didn't comment. Hell, it looked like a regular penis to me.

Mark began to stroke the shaft of his penis. "Don't forget about your boy over here."

"Don't worry, you'll join us in round two," Alana assured him.

"That's what I'm talking about," Mark said as he sat back down and continued to stroke his penis with his right hand and sip from his drink with his left.

I looked at Alana as she slowly pulled off her shirt to reveal a beautiful purple paisley bra. She bent down over me and kissed me on my neck, then whispered, "I wore this for you."

Alana sat up and straddled me. I reached up and began to caress her breasts then slid my hands down to her stomach and in between her legs. Alana slid down on top of me as she separated my legs with hers and we began to grind. We continued to kiss and grind our bodies moving in a sensual unison, then Alana whispered, "Take off your panties, Kai." I did without so much as a moment's hesitation. I hated how much I liked Alana, hated how much control she had over me – but as I watched her at that moment, I realized she had control over Mark, as well.

Alana reached over and grabbed a small bottle sitting on the table next to us. She looked at Mark, then back at me. "I got us some flavored liquid gel. It heats up," Alana said as she simultaneously snapped open the top and drizzled the warm liquid on my bare stomach and breast in a circular pattern. She then bent down and began to slowly lick the gel off of my stomach and breasts. Then she quickly and without much hesitation made her way down between my thighs and began eating me out with such aggression, I didn't know what had come over her. She was never this rough or fast, and even though I came in mere seconds, it wasn't her. Alana always liked attention and being the center of it, and she was working every angle.

Alana sat up and signaled for Mark to come and join us. He was hella tipsy but ready to take part in every man's fantasy, so he didn't waste any time and began kissing Alana from behind, then slowly pulled off her panties and entered her from behind.

"Oh, baby, you feel so good," Alana moaned in pleasure as she reached out for me, pulling me towards her as she began to kiss me. I felt weird and very much out of place once again as Alana tried to keep me included, but the more intense the sex got with Mark, the further I was from her mind. Alana was in a different world right now, one that didn't include me. I slowly slid away as I watched the woman I thought I loved being screwed by someone else, I didn't like it, not one bit. Everything was feeling wrong about this relationship and I knew I had to make it right.

I had to kick my habit before everything in my life came to a crashing halt.

30 · TURNING POINT

"KAI, WAKE UP, IT'S your brother!" The sound of Todd's voice jolted me out of my deep sleep.

"What?" I asked, trying to make sense of what I'd half-heard as I sat up in my bed. The room was dark as I struggled to focus on Todd's face. I glanced at the clock: 3am.

"Your brother, he's in the hospital," Todd said.

"What happened?" I mumbled, rubbing my eyes.

"They found Raymond unconscious at the shelter he was living in," Todd said. "They think it was a drug overdose."

"What hospital is he in?" I asked.

"He's at County," Todd said as he stood and began throwing on his jeans and a sweatshirt. I shook off the last bit of sleep and quickly dressed. We left immediately for the hospital.

I loved how supportive Todd always was when it came to my brother; he never minded helping out whenever he could.

Other guys that I dated in the past always had a problem with Raymond – or, should I say, my involvement in my brother's chaotic life – but not Todd. He was there whenever I needed him and never complained once.

Todd and I arrived at the hospital within half a hour. I wasn't sure if I would find my brother dead or alive. I thought I was prepared for anything at that moment, but when I saw Corrine sitting in the waiting room, I realized that I was not prepared for that.

"Hey, Corrine, what are you doing here?" I asked as I slowly sat down next to her in the crowded waiting room.

"The shelter called me. Apparently Raymond listed both of our names as his emergency contacts," Corrine said.

I stayed with my mother as Todd went to get us coffee. "So, how is he?" I asked, still trying to wake up.

"I don't know, they haven't really said anything yet."

"Does dad know you're here?" I asked.

"No, he doesn't," Corrine answered.

I knew it was a big deal for my mother to be there. In spite of the hardship that Raymond's addiction had brought to my mothers life, in the end, Raymond Edwards was still her son and no amount of hurt and disappointment could erase the love of her first and only son.

"He's trying, ya know, he wants to stop but he just needs our help," I said. I always picked my words carefully when discussing Raymond.

Corrine was silent, then she turned to me. "I don't know what to do about Raymond, I really don't," she said. "He's slipped so far into this dark place and I don't know how to pull him out of it."

My mother began to shake her head. "Where did I go wrong with him?" She dropped her head as she worked hard to hold back her tears. I placed my hand on hers, feeling the softness in her touch and the pain she felt in her heart.

"Mom, you can't dwell on the past," I said, "so let's just

focus on the here and now and how we can help him through this."

I couldn't believe how strong I sounded when it came to fixing Raymond's life. Of course, when it came to my own I was clueless.

"He wants to give rehab another shot," I told her, "but I can't afford it and, well, Mila won't help. I know he has been down that path a few times, but maybe we just have to keep trying until it sticks. I know that one day he will get through rehab and come out on the other side."

Corrine closed her eyes. My guess was that she needed to process everything that was going on. I looked up to see Todd coming our way. I gave him a look, a look to let him know we were having the "Raymond talk." Todd did a quick turn and headed around the corner before Corrine even realized what was happening.

"I will pay for his rehab," she said. My mother opened her eyes and turned toward me. "I can't continue to turn my back on my son, or any of my children, for that matter. Despite the lives that you all live, you're still my babies and I love you all unconditionally."

I wondered if my mom was trying to tell me something, indirectly of course, about my own life, the secret life that I had been living for too long. I shook off that thought and focused all my attention back onto the subject at hand, my brother.

"I know, Mom," I said as tears welled up in my eyes. I knew Raymond had a long road ahead of him, but I also knew that he was going to be okay, he had us.

31 · LET'S BE REAL

I WAS ON MY way to meet Alana for a late lunch, per her rre-
quest. Apparently, there was something she was dying to tell
me that was too important to be said over the phone. I was
exhausted. My nights were still filled with the same nightmares
that haunted my world. I needed to find a way to make them
stop, while at the same time acknowledging that they once
existed.

As I headed down Michigan Avenue, I reminded myself
that it had been a month since I said I would break up with
Alana – and I was still with her. Every time I tried to form the
words to say it, she would say (or do!) something that would
change my mind; I needed to find the strength, but I didn't
know where to look.

I arrived in front of Coy restaurant and took a deep breath.
I stared at my reflection in the glass double door with gold

trim, and reminded my emotions that this affair I was having was just that, an affair; I shouldn't let things get to me like they do, but they always did and I hated that. My feelings for Alana were growing stronger each day and I hated the way it made me feel. I wasn't in control of my emotions, in control of my life. It was starting to take a toll.

I arrived at Coy to find Alana sitting in the back. She was chatting on her cell phone as she excitedly waved me over. I acknowledged her wave and headed in her direction. I sat down without a greeting of any kind. She winked at me, her way of saying hello, as she wrapped up her phone conversation. She said her goodbyes and snapped her phone closed.

"Hey, you look adorable today," Alana said as she dropped her phone in the burnt orange leather purse hanging on her chair.

"Thanks." Although I was just thinking, on my way over to meet her, that I looked rather tired, I had to conclude that everything was relative. Alana looked like she had a glow. I was not sure why, but I was sure that I would soon find out.

"So what's the big emergency that you just had to see me?" I asked, trying find out why I was there.

A huge grin engulfed Alana's face as she leaned forward. "Victoria's Secret wants to shoot me for their spring bathing suit line," she said with immense excitement in her voice.

"Can you believe that, Kai? My agent called me yesterday to tell me. It's not one hundred percent official but who cares, showing an interest is good enough for me."

"That's great," I said. I wanted to be happy for Alana as I squeezed out an "I'm happy for you smile" but I knew it was nowhere near convincing.

Alana sat back and gave me a look. "Kai, aren't you happy for me?"

"Yeah, I,um, yeah, I am."

Alana tilted her head to the left as she raised an eyebrow. "That was real convincing."

"No, really – I am," I said. Actually, I really was happy for her in a career sense; the problem was that I always got irritated with her when it came to situations that affected us.

"Well, you don't look happy. What's wrong with you?" Alana asked as she placed her hand on my arm. I quickly pulled it away as if I'd been touched by something hot.

"Wow, what is wrong with you?" Alana repeated.

"Nothing," I said as I looked away.

"Kai, my touching your arm in public is not a sign that we're 'together' or anything."

"That's not it," I said.

"Then what is it?"

I shifted in my seat, and couldn't believe I was about to express my feelings, my insecurities, my irritations – all of which were festering from a habit that had formed between us lately, or should I say, a habit that was forming with Alana.

"Are you going to tell me what the problem is?" Alana asked.

I took a deep breath. "It's us."

"'Us'?" Alana asked.

"Yes, Alana, 'us.' I waited for you last night and you never showed up."

Alana looked confused, almost if I were making something up. "Waited for me? For what?" Alana asked.

I leaned forward, making sure she would hear every little, irritated syllable that came out of my mouth. "The movies," I said. "We had plans, remember?"

Irritated, Alana took a deep breath, then spoke in a very calm, nonchalant tone. "Kai, I had a date last night."

I looked Alana dead in her eyes. "We had a date last night!" I said, trying as hard as I could to keep my emotions in check.

Alana shrugged her shoulders and continued with the same tone. "Well, I guess I forgot."

"Yeah, that was pretty obvious," I said, this time not so

calmly.

Alana sat back and crossed her arms as a smirk slowly crawled across her face. "Kai, I said I forgot, what's the big deal?"

"The big deal is you could have called."

"Yeah, I could have... but I didn't," she said matter-of-fact-ly.

"Hm," was all I could muster up for a response. I took a deep breath and then another. Alana was raking my last nerve.

"Listen, Kai, I know we are messing around, but let's face the facts," Alana said in her shittyist voice ever, which felt like ten bees stinging me all at one time. "We're not a couple, Kai, and I don't have to answer to you."

Alana and locked eyes after that comment for a few moments. It felt like it lasted a lifetime. And in those few moments I realized that I was in too deep. I knew that I was slowly sliding down a slippery slope without any means of stopping, or a way to pull myself back up. I also knew that I had to dig my heels in and pull myself out immediately, before I disappeared in that emotional black hole. I needed to face the fact that I had a boyfriend, but more importantly, I needed to start acting like it.

"I'd better go," I said as I grabbed my purse, stood and headed out the restaurant. I could have stayed and attempted to talk it out with Alana, but why? She had made it abundantly clear that she didn't give a damn about what we had together, and it was time I started acting the same way.

I heard Alana call my name a few times but I continued to walk, never turning back, not once.

32 · RESTLESS MOMENT

MY HEAD WAS SPINNING. I couldn't get my conversation with Alana out of my mind. "We're not a couple, Kai, we're not a couple." And she was right, we weren't a couple. Then why did I feel like shit, and why did I feel like I'd just had a fight with my boyfriend?

I glanced over at the clock. It was 4am. Then I turned to look at Todd, who was fast asleep. I slowly peeled the blankets back from my body and carefully slid out the bed, trying not to wake Todd. There was no sense in my tossing and turning and waking him up. I snatched up my navy blue sweatsuit, socks, and gym shoes, and headed out of the bedroom and out of the condo. I decided to take a walk, clear my mind, and figure some things out. I headed down to a 24-hour café to grab a cup of coffee and a very early breakfast. The air was refreshingly cool as the early morning dew hung in the air. The birds chirped a familiar melody reminding me that daylight was only a few hours away.

As I sat in the café staring out of the window, I couldn't help but wonder why Alana had such a hold over me. Was I in love with her, or was it just infatuation? The longer I was with Alana, the more I would ask myself, "Do I want to be with a woman, or is this something that I am just experimenting with?" My feelings had to be somewhat real, because I felt a pull towards Alana, but at the same time I yearned to be with the man I loved.

I dropped my head into my hands. I had never been attracted to a woman before, so why then and why her? The door of the café opened and two women entered. They walked over and sat at a booth about ten feet from me. Any other time they would have been nothing to focus on, two girlfriends having an early morning breakfast. But these women were different, their body language said they were more than just friends, I could tell after a few minutes of observing them that they were lovers. They sat on the same side of the table, and one woman was very feminine while the other was a little more masculine. They talked with their hands and I watched as they whispered and giggled with each other.

It was obvious that these two women were not only lovers but very open about their sexuality, something that was very foreign to me. I tried not to stare, but at the same time I was intrigued by their presence. I thought about my relationship with Alana and how when we were out in public I was constantly wondering if people knew, if people could tell that we were together. It bothered me when someone would look at us too long, or make a comment about us after a long stare, not knowing what they were saying. I continued to watch these women and wondered if I could live that life, be one of those women. What I concluded was, "No, I don't want that life, I don't want what those women shared, I want a life with Todd."

So why was I so hesitant to let Alana go? Why was I so vulnerable around her? Todd represented everything I ever wanted in my life, but at the same time he could never touch me the way that Alana did and vice versa.

I finished my breakfast and headed back home. It was nearing 5am and the sun was rising over a ten-story brick building in front of me. I knew it was time to end it with Alana; in my heart of hearts I knew this particular situation was not right. I knew that my feelings for her were strong; I just didn't know why I had them.

33 · CHANGING FACES

I TOLD MY ASSISTANT to hold all my calls unless it was Todd, my masseuse, or information about Raymond. I hadn't spoken to Alana in a few days, and even though it was probably for the best, it was bothering me. I couldn't seem to shake her from my thoughts. I was doing more than I probably needed to do just to keep my mind occupied – and it worked, so well, in fact, that I didn't even realize when Corrine was standing in my office.

"Hey, what are you doing here?" I asked as I glanced behind Corrine to see my assistant five feet behind her with an "I just couldn't stop her" look. By the expression on her face I knew Corrine had something she wanted to talk about. When the subject matter was pressing enough, Corrine never gave any warning when she really needed to talk. She just showed up and barged in. She never wanted to give the unwary listener a chance to escape.

I had to choose my words wisely as I wasn't exactly sure why she was there. "Is Raymond okay?" I inquired.

"He's fine."

"So when does he start rehab?" I asked.

"I believe in a few days, but I'm not here to talk about Raymond," Corrine said as she sauntered over to a chair directly across from me, then sat and quickly crossed her legs. "Mila called me this morning."

My stomach did a somersault with a back double dismount. I knew at that moment what was in store. No wonder Corrine hadn't called before just dropping by; she had a bone to pick with me. I should have figured Mila had to tell someone, and since it couldn't be Todd, the next best bet would be my mom. "Corrine, before you say anything, I just want to say –"

My mom put up her hand. "Kai, honey, it's okay. I'm not mad"

"That – what?" I asked with a mixture of relief and disbelief in my voice. "You're not?"

"Not at all."

I shifted in my chair, trying to figure out what the hell was going on. I wasn't totally convinced yet that my mother was completely informed, not at all.

"So you're – disappointed?" I asked.

"Nope, not that either," Corinne said.

I sat up and leaned a bit closer to my mom. "Okay, are we talking about the same thing here?"

"Yes, I believe so," she replied.

"Good. So are you going to tell me what it is?" I wanted to make sure we were on the same page, although at the same time I was holding my breath.

"Your relationship with Alana, or should I say your intimate relationship," Corrine said as she tilted her head to the left and leaned back.

I let out that deep breath I had just pulled in. "Right," I

said hesitantly. There really was nothing else to say; I was out of words.

There was an awkward silence for a few moments, and once again I felt exposed, felt vulnerable. And even though my mom just said she was not mad or disappointed, it was the fact that she knew, knew something about me that I would rather have kept personal. "When did you figure it out?" I asked

"The moment she walked in my house," Corrine said.

"You did?" I asked.

"I did."

"Wow!"

"Mothers know everything," said Corinne. "I pride myself on knowing more."

"How did you know?" I asked.

"Let's just call it a mother's intuition."

"Right," I said as I sat back in my chair, wondering what would come out of my mother's mouth next. My guess was something very awkward.

"So how long have you two been seeing each other?" she asked.

Bingo! "Not that long, really," I said.

"What's not long? Three months, one month?" she asked.

"I'm not sure, I wasn't really keeping track." I couldn't believe I was having this conversation with my own mother – Miss Pristine, Miss Conservative, Miss I-will-throw-myself-under-a-bus-to-get-my-daughter-married – and that she was okay with my relationship with a woman.

"Sweetheart," Corinne said, "we all experiment in our lives. I think it is a way of finding oneself."

"You do?" I said slowly.

"I do," she answered, "but just understand that, in those times of experimentation, we have to be careful of who's involved and, more importantly, who might get hurt."

I knew exactly where my mom was going, but at the same time I just couldn't tell her how being in this relationship with

Alana would only hurt the one I truly love, and that is Todd.

As I listened to my mom talk I had the irresistible urge to pinch my forearm to make sure I wasn't in the middle of just a bad dream. Deep down I was hoping it was.

"So, I'm sure Mila had an earful to say," I said, feeling a lot more relaxed, one indication being the sweat spots under my arm were starting to dry up.

"Mila needs to mind her own business," Corinne said. "Besides, she needs to stay focused on her life and leave yours to you."

Amen to that I exclaimed silently! "Mom, I just have to say, you are blowing me away right now, and I never thought you would be okay with this."

Corrine smiled, stood up, then looked at her watch. Apparently I was just one of many stops on her busy agenda that day. She grabbed her purse and walked over to my side of the desk.

"I know you may think I am a stick in the mud, or even a bit judgmental sometimes, but I could tell you a few stories," Corrine said as she turned and headed for the door. She was about to exit, then quickly turned back towards me to say, "By the way, nice shoes. I used to have a similar pair back in the day." Corrine gave me a very knowing look and a wink. She smiled softly and walked out of my office.

I fell back into my leather chair as a smile crawled across my face, and at that moment I realized that my mother, despite all of my preconceived notions about her, had walked in the same shoes as mine.

34 · THE PROPOSAL OF A LIFETIME

I FELT MYSELF SLOWLY drifting to sleep when I felt Todd get up from the couch. "Where are you going?" I asked groggily.

"To get something to drink."

"Can you get me more wine, please?" I asked.

"Like you need it! You're already sleeping."

"I'm up, really," I said, pulling myself upright on the couch."Not for long," Todd said as he winked at me and headed to the kitchen. I glanced at the clock; it was 10:30pm. Sleepless in Seattle was almost over, although it didn't matter since we had seen the movie countless times this year alone. One of the secrets that Todd revealed to me when we first met was that his favorite movie of all time was Sleepless in Seattle, but if I ever brought that up in front of his homeboys, colleagues, or siblings, he would deny it. But alone with me, he would watch it over and over again.

188 · MY MAN'S BEST FRIEND

Todd walked back into the living room with a glass of wine for me and a beer for himself. He glanced over at me as he handed me my wine.

"You want me to rewind the movie?" I asked, feeling wide awake all of a sudden. My second wind had just kicked in and I knew I could stay awake for another hour or so.

"No, I'm good," Todd said as he took a swig of his beer, and then placed it on the table in front of us. I sipped on my wine, feeling a slightly different energy from Todd, but I couldn't put my finger on it. Todd just stared at me, then smiled.

"Are you okay, baby?" I asked as I placed my hand on his leg.

Todd just looked intensely at me. It started to make me feel a bit uneasy at first. Then he leaned over and gently kissed me on the forehead, nose, and finally the lips. He sat back on the couch, never taking his eyes off of me. He looked back at the television, then grabbed the remote and clicked the TV off. Todd shifted his body towards me.

"Are you committed to me?" he asked.

Although a simple and direct question, for some reason I was a little taken aback.

"Yes, baby, I am," I said.

"I mean, are you 100% totally committed to me?" Todd asked again, this time a little more intensely.

Now I was starting to get scared, thinking Todd was playing a trick. Had someone blown my cover? I thought about my mom, Mila, and maybe even Alana. I felt the back of my neck getting warm and the palms of my hands began to perspire. "Why are you asking me this, Todd?"

"Because I have to know. Are you?"

I took a deep breath,. "Yes, I am, 100%."

Todd continued to stare at me then a huge smile came over his face, as if he'd felt a surge of relief. "That's good to hear, because I am committed to you, too, and I just wanted to make that clear before I did what I am about to do."

Todd took a deep breath as he pulled out a small black box, and before I had a chance to register exactly what was going on, He opened the box and right in front of my eyes was a beautiful brilliant-cut, 2-carat diamond ring shining up at me – and it was all mine.

I was speechless, shocked, elated.

"Oh, my God, Todd!"

He took the ring out the box and placed it on my finger. "Kai Edwards, will you marry me?"

I looked at Todd and he had tears in his eyes, and at that moment the guilt I had been suppressing for the last six months came rushing to the forefront of my being. I knew this was my last chance to say something, to come clean, to start this new chapter of my life off on the right track. My heart was pounding at the anticipation of revealing the truth, the whole truth, and nothing but. I was frantically looking for an 'in' to tell Todd everything, but how would I start, how would I explain these last several months, how would he take it? Most importantly, how would I explain the 'why'? Why Alana, why his best friend, and why now?

I swallowed hard and glanced down at that beautiful ring that was now on my left ring finger, and almost immediately I felt a sense of peace and security that overpowered me. I didn't want that feeling to go away, not in that moment, not in my lifetime.

I looked up at Todd and a huge smile broke across my face. "Yes, I will marry you."

"Yes!!!" Todd exclaimed as he grabbed me and hugged me ever so tightly.

"I love you," I said.

"I love you more," Todd retorted.

I kissed Todd like I'd never kissed him before, and right then I knew that something had to change. I had found that buried strength I needed to break it off with Alana – and when I did, I would bury what we shared in the same deep, dark place.

35 · RULES OF ENGAGEMENT

MY MOTHER DECIDED TO have an engagement party for Todd and me, and of course I could not say no. It was something I knew she had been planning in her head for years. Even if I had thought about telling her no, to her that would've meant, "Not right now, but maybe later in the month," so I just sat back and let Corrine do her thing.

There were 150 people on the invite list and I probably knew about 20 of them. For the first time in the history of my mother's extravagance, I did not mind that, especially since she was footing the bill. She could invite the Queen of England for all I cared. Corrine was working overtime to make sure everything would be perfect. Not a detail was left unattended, from the food to the flowers to the parting gifts.

I arrived at my parent's house early, just to see how everything was turning out, but mostly to get approval from Corrine

192 · MY MAN'S BEST FRIEND

on the outfit that I had picked out. I was wearing a black dress with quarter length sleeves. The dress was form fitted at the top and flared just slightly from waist down to just above my knee. I accented my pick with a pair of knee high form fitting Jimmy Choo boots.

I entered the house to the smell of fresh flowers. I walked into the kitchen to open a new bottle of wine when I noticed Mila starting to do the same thing. I had not laid eyes on my twin sister since our last confrontation, if you could call it that. I was secretly hoping that Mila would pass on coming to my engagement party. But I knew she would not miss the opportunity to show up.

Upon entering the kitchen, the air was awkward and noticeably silent between me and my twin sister. I busied myself by opening a bottle of merlot and pouring a healthy sized glassful. I didn't really have anything to say to her – and I was hoping the feeling was mutual. Unfortunately, I was wrong.

"So is it going to be a double wedding?" Mila snickered as she took a sip of her wine. She was clearly already tipsy and looking to start a fight.

I tried my best to ignore Mila, but of course Mila was not having it, so she just kept coming at me. "So where is your girl-friend anyway, was she too heartbroken to show up?" Mila sneered, her words aggravating me to no end. I thought about taking the high road and walking right out of the kitchen, but then it dawned on me that the high road was for people who were afraid to speak their minds.

The fact is, when it came to Mila, I had a lot on my mind.

I took a deep breath, turned to face Mila and looked at her directly in the eyes while taking two steps closer to her.

"You know what, Mila?" I began. "Sometimes you just need to shut up." I confidently walked over to the kitchen door and closed it abruptly. There was no need for my guest to hear what I was about to unleash on my sister. Mila took a step back almost as if in retreat to my gestures indicating it was about to go down.

Either way, I didn't care; I had to say what I needed to say. "You know why I don't tell you anything about my life?" I continued. "Because when you find out something about people, you always use it against them."

"Is that what you think?" she asked.

"No, Mila, that's what I know. Yes, I had an affair with a woman and, yes, she was my man's best friend. But it doesn't make me less of a person," I said forcefully, "it just makes me human – and sometimes, Mila, humans make mistakes."

Mila stared at me with a stoic glare, but I was not about to let her intimidate me, not then, not when I had too much that I still had to say.

"Bottom line, Mila, you live in your big house with your fancy cars and your money to burn," I said, "but your husband doesn't come home and you're unhappy. Because of that, if you can make a person feel like shit by focusing on their less-than-ideal situation, you will do just that – but only to make yourself feel better, in hopes of getting through one more day of your miserable life."

Mila continued to give me a blank stare as I circled her like my prey.

"But guess what Mila?" I challenged her. "I'm not going to be your target anymore. I know I'm not perfect, I know I've made my choices and mistakes in life. But overall I'm pretty happy. I have a few regrets. And that kills you, it really does, because you are not happy."

By this time, Mila was quiet, and seemed to be at a loss for words – for once.

I knew it was time for my exit, so I turned and headed toward the door, passing Mila along the way. Before leaving, I quickly turned back around to face my twin sister.

I looked her right in the eye again. "I don't hate you, Mila. I just feel sorry for you. I feel sorry you are missing out on the life you won't allow yourself to live."

I exited the kitchen, and for the first time, I could recall, I felt pretty damn good after talking to Mila.

I didn't feel like joining the party, at least not right then. I needed time to cool off, so I headed upstairs to the family den, a quiet place to sit and think. I closed my eyes but a few minutes later I felt someone standing over me. I opened my eyes to see that it was Alana. "Congratulations," Alana said as she smiled down at me.

"Thanks," I said cautiously, "but how did you know I was up here?"

"I was just walking in when I saw you heading up the stairs, so after I said my hello's I headed up here, too. Kind of figured you'd be in here," Alana said as she sat down next to me on the sofa.

Alana pulled my left hand close to examine the ring.

"Yep, that's the one," she said.

"What do you mean, 'that's the one'?"

"The one I picked out," Alana said.

"You picked out?" I retorted as I pulled my hand out of her grip.

"Well, helped pick out, I should say."

"Alana, why did you have anything at all to do with picking out my ring?"

"Because you should have seen the ring Todd was going to get for you. You're lucky I intervened," Alana said as she continued to admire the ring.

I didn't know whether to be pissed or happy that Alana had picked out my ring – okay, helped pick out my ring – but the more I thought about it, the happier I was, because I truly loved the ring.

"You did a good job," I said

"Thanks," Alana replied. "Of course, Todd had the final say."

"Well, I would hope so." We held a stare. "So you knew he

was going to propose?" I asked.

"Of course," she said. "I am his best friend, although I didn't think it would be this soon."

"Well, we have been dating for a while now," I said.

"I know, but Todd tends to drag his feet with things, always wants everything to be perfect," Alana said as she leaned back, turning her head to look at me. We held a stare that lingered a moment. "I miss you." Alana leaned in to kiss me, but I pulled away.

"Alana, the last time we kissed in my parents' house, Mila saw us."

"So?"

"So," I said firmly, "she has been giving me the third degree ever since, not to mention that, well, we need to set some boundaries now."

"Boundaries?" Alana asked.

"Yes, boundaries, especially now that I'm engaged," I said. I knew that what I should have been saying was that Todd and I were engaged, that my affair with her was over – but the "boundaries" line escaped from my mouth instead.

Alana looked at me as a smile spread across her face. She chuckled. "Right, boundaries. I'm gonna get another drink. You want one?"

"Alana," I said, "I'm serious."

"Yeah, okay," Alana said, standing. "I'll see you downstairs."

"I'm not done talking about this," I said.

"Okay, I'll see you downstairs," Alana said again as she exited the room, leaving me alone with my thoughts. It was clear that Alana was not taking me seriously.

It was definitely time to break it off with her.

36 · MOVIN' ON WITHOUT 'CHA

ALANA WENT OUT OF town for a few weeks to shoot the Victoria's Secret swimsuit issue. This was perfect timing as I really needed the space and the time to think my situation over. It was obvious Alana hadn't taken me seriously when I'd told her about us needing boundaries, so I decided I needed to tell her again, and I wasn't taking "no" for an answer this time.

After she returned home, I texted Alana to see if she were available to stop by my office. It took her about an hour to get back to me, but her response was, 'Yes'.

I was deep into work when my assistant buzzed me to let me know that Alana had arrived. I was a little bit nervous, but wasn't going to let it show. Alana entered without even saying hello. I could tell she was irritated and I knew why; my avoidance never sat well with her, even from the beginning, but she knew why I was that way, especially at this difficult time. Alana had the biggest ego of any woman that I had ever known. And because I had a man, she felt that she had a free pass to do whatever she wanted. She often forgot that I still had feelings.

Alana sat in front of me silently as we both tried to decipher each other's thoughts. She looked away, down toward her purse as if seeing it for the first time, and then finally broke the silence. "So, why haven't you been returning my phone calls or texts?"

Alana looked up and stared directly in my eyes as I said, "I needed time to think, Alana."

"Think about what?"

"About us," I said, "and how we have to have boundaries now that I'm engaged."

Alana dropped back into her chair. "You're really serious about this 'boundary thing,' I see."

"Alana, I'm engaged now," I said, stressing each word.

"And that's supposed to mean something?" she asked.

"It means a lot. I don't want to enter into a marriage like this," I said.

"Like what, Kai?

"Cheating on my husband with you," I said.

"Well," Alana replied, "maybe you should have thought about that before you started fucking me."

"Listen, Alana, I don't want to fight, I just want to make sure we are still cool."

"You tell me. Are we?"

"Why are you making this so complicated?" I asked her.

"Why are you acting like you have morals now?" she shot back.

AlI didn't know why she was making this so difficult. I knew I had to come on harder for her to understand exactly where I stood, even if I did come off as a hypocrite.

"Bottom line, Alana, Todd's the future and you – well, you were just fun."

Alana shot me a wide eyed look and her eyebrows almost

touched her hairline.

If looks could kill I would have been oh-so-dead.

"Fun?" Alana repeated.

I took a deep breath. "Yeah, Alana, you were just fun. Besides, we're not a couple, remember that?"

Alana just stared at me, not saying a word, but had I looked closely I probably would have seen smoke rising from the back of her neck. All my pent-up anger toward her was dissipating with each syllable I spoke. My insecurities, jealousy, and strong need to feel vindicated were all being released. I looked away from Alana's intense stare. Then I heard Alana chuckle.

"You're right, Kai, I'm tripping," she said. "You should put Todd first. I guess I just wasn't ready to lose you."

I was at a loss for words, not expecting that to come out of Alana's mouth, at least not this soon. "You okay then?"

"Yeah, I'm fine. I don't want to fight about this," Alana stated calmly.

"I don't either," I said. "I just really need to change some things in my life, and I just hope you can understand that now."

"I guess I didn't really take you seriously when you said you needed boundaries," said Alana, "and I'm sorry. It's just that I miss you."

Just hearing those three words gave me a warm fluttery feeling in my stomach. "I miss you too," I returned.

Alana walked over to me. I felt myself getting weaker with every passing moment. She stared at me closely and took my hand. She leaned in and kissed me passionately on the cheek.

"Can I at least have you one last time?" she pleaded softly.

I felt her soft breath on my face, her lips inches away from mine. I wanted to kiss her but I just couldn't. I had to stay strong. "We can't, I can't, Alana," I said as I pulled away. "You'd better go, please."

"You really want me to leave?" she asked.

We hold a stare. "Yes," I said softly but convincingly.

"Your wish is my command," Alana said. She reached down and grabbed her purse."Bye, Kai," she said as she headed out my office.

•

You did what?" Simone asked, looking up from her laptop. I had headed straight to Simone's office the moment Alana had left mine.

"It was time, ya know," I said. "I can't keep seeing her. Besides, how would I look married with a significant other on the side?"

"Like 85 percent of the population, 80 percent of that being men, of course."

I glared at Simone disapprovingly.

"What?" she responded defensively. "You asked. But honestly, honey, this is for the best. If you really feel you want to be with Todd, then cutting off Alana is the best thing. Lord knows I'm not one to stop anyone from having fun, especially when it's the horizontal kind. But fucking Alana was a little bit too close to home."

I knew Simone was right, but I was still having a hard time with my decision, mainly because my feelings for Alana had grown and now – well, now I had to just cut them off. I thought about how it would be when I finally saw her again, if she would just act as if nothing happened, or if there would be some awkwardness. I wondered if she would even bother showing up for my wedding.

"So how do you feel?" Simone asked.

"Overwhelmed. I need to take a trip."

"A trip where?" Simone asked.

"I don't know," I answered. "Hawaii, Mexico, Bahamas, you name it, I just need to get away. Sandy white beaches, sunshine, and piña coladas or a strawberry daiquiri sound real good right about now."

"That sounds like a great idea," Simone said, "not to mention you could use some R&R and some quality time with Todd. We're done with the 'Just B' campaign and our new project isn't scheduled to start for a few weeks, so –".

"Do you think I should call Alana?" I asked, switching gears and not knowing why I even said that.

"Negative," Simone said quickly. "You two need some space right now. Thank God we're done using her, it wouldn't be good for business to have her around now that you two are Splitsville and all. Not to mention, I really didn't care too much for her as a model."

"You didn't? Why?" I asked.

"Don't get me wrong," said Simone. "She's beautiful, but her weight fluctuated too much for me. How many times did we have to get her jeans resized? A lot of the budget went into her wardrobe each week."

"Well," I said, "that's in the past, along with my sneaking around."

"I know you're relieved about that," Simone said.

"Yeah, I am, but I think one day I will tell Todd, when I know that he will be okay with it."

"Be careful about that, Kai, because a lot of men are not okay with it, especially when they find out that they were at the park but not invited to play in the sandbox," Simone said, emphasizing 'sandbox' with her inimitable air quotes.

I smiled, thinking how right Simone was. "I'd better go."

"Where are you going?" Simone asked.

"I have a trip to plan," I said.

"Oh, that's right the post-breakup, pre-engagement trip," Simone said with a sarcastic tone and a huge grin.

"Shut it!"

"Never! But I love you too, darlin'," Simone said.

I headed out of Simone's office as she switched right back into work mode. As I walked back to my office, I couldn't help but wonder what was going through Alana's head right at that moment. Was she mad, sad, or just indifferent? My cell phone rang and I looked down at the display to see that Alana was calling. I stared at her name as my phone played out the ring, then quickly sent her call into voicemail.

Simone was right. What was the point of talking to her now? It was time to move on.

202 · MY MAN'S BEST FRIEND

37 · TOO LITTLE TOO LATE

I WAS EXCITED TO tell Todd the news about our Caribbean cruise for two. In less than a month we would be sailing the beautiful blue seas to destinations such as Barbados, Jamaica and the Bahamas. I couldn't wait. I figured our honeymoon wouldn't be for a year or so, so the timing of this trip was perfect. I hoped Todd would be just as excited as I was.I finished up at work so I could head home to surprise him. I couldn't believe that I did something so spontaneous and daring. I grabbed our tickets and itinerary from my top left drawer that my travel agent Linda FedEx'd over first thing that morning. I'd told her that I needed this trip planned ASAP. It would be a pre-wedding celebration that we both wouldn't forget. So Linda hooked it up just as I'd expected her to.

I arrived home around 7:30 in the evening. As I walked through the front door, I could see the light reflecting on the hardwood indicating Todd was in his office. I'd stopped at the corner market to pick up some fresh tilapia, salad, and a bottle of merlot. I set the bags on the counter and began to unpack the items when Todd walked up behind me. I turned around when I felt his presence. He stood there staring at me for a second. His face was hard, almost emotionless.

"Hey, baby," I said as I walked over and planted a kiss on his lips. "I have a surprise for you."

Todd was stiff and didn't return my affection.

"Are you okay?" I asked as I turned and started putting the groceries away. "I picked up dinner. I thought we could stay in tonight and I would cook."

Todd still didn't respond but walked over to the fridge, pulled out a bottle of water and took a gulp. He slowly placed the bottle down on the counter and turned back to face me.

"Baby what's wrong with you?" I asked as I grabbed the bottle of wine to open it.

Todd picked up the water bottle again, taking another gulp. "I know about you and Alana," he said.

Upon hearing those words I gasped, as if someone had drop-kicked me in the stomach, knocking all the wind out of me. I didn't even realize the bottle of wine had slipped from my hand until I heard it shatter on the floor.

Todd and I locked eyes and, even though I knew what he meant, I couldn't bring myself to admit it, at least not out loud. "What, what do you mean?" I replied with a slight stutter.

Todd took another swig from his water, and then unexpectedly threw the bottle across the room. It hit the wall and water splattered everywhere. "I think you know exactly what I mean, Kai," Todd shouted.

My body tensed as my breathing started to become erratic. I felt dizzy and lightheaded. Time stood still and everything in the room became crystal clear – the dripping faucet, the ticking clock, the humming sound of the refrigerator. I couldn't speak; I was paralyzed inside and out.

Todd began to slowly walk towards me. He spoke slowly but firmly. "She told me everything, every fucking detail of what went down."

As he stepped forward, I mirrored his steps backwards.

"She even said you initiated the whole thing," he continued.

"What? No, she's lying, she, she initiated it not me."

"Oh really," Todd said. "Well her story sounded pretty convincing."

"She's lying," I insisted. "You have to believe me."

"Believe you? Why in the hell would I believe you now?" Todd asked as his voice started getting louder. "You've been lying in my face for eight fucking months and now you want me to believe you? It's a little too late for that."

I couldn't believe this was happening, I couldn't believe Alana had blindsided me like that. We had a goddamn pact and that bitch broke it. How could I have been so fucking stupid to trust her?

"Baby, let me explain, please," I pleaded, making my way towards Todd. I touched his arm, trying to calm him down. Todd snapped his arm away from me. "Don't fucking touch me."

I wanted to die, right then, right there.

"I knew there was something up with you," he said slowly. "I felt it, I just never thought it was with, with Alana."

"I was going to tell you, I really was."

"Really? When Kai? When were you going to tell me that you were fucking my best friend, huh? When?"

"I, I…" I couldn't get the words out, but I needed something new to say, something that would wipe that hurtful look off his face, but I was lost. I had lost.

"I want you out of here," he said.

"Todd, please let me explain."

"Explain what? How you cheated on me? How you lied to me? How you looked me in my face and told me there was no one else?"

"Baby," I said, "I asked you if being with a girl was cheating and you said no."

Todd looked at me and shook his head. "But you were fucking my best friend, and that goes beyond the fact that she was a girl."

I reached out to Todd again, but he pulled away as he placed his hands on top of his head and began to walk in circles around the kitchen island. We can talk this out," I said.

"There's nothing to talk about," Todd replied, "so just leave."

"Todd – "

"I'm serious Kai," he said, raising his voice. "Get out!"

I paused for a minute, I wanted to make one last plea but it was apparent that it would fall on deaf ears. "Fine, I'll go."

I bent down and started picking up the glass from the shattered bottle.

"Leave it," Todd said.

I stopped what I was doing and slowly stood as we locked eyes one more time.

"You should have told me, I shouldn't have had to heard this from her, not from Alana," Todd said in a soft and hurtful tone. He gave me one last look before he headed out the kitchen.

I stood there, unable to move, unable to breathe, unable to cry. I was angry, hurt and confused. I felt an intense sense of betrayal toward Alana that I had never felt toward any human being before in my life.

I guess I knew right then how Alana had felt about our breakup. I just never thought in a million years she would have blindsided me like she did. But you never really know a person until you cross them or challenge their ego – or, in Alana's case, strip her control from a relationship.

I grabbed my purse and headed out the door. I figured I would send Simone back later for my things.

206 · MY MAN'S BEST FRIEND

38 · TOO DARK TO SEE

I MOVED MOST OF my essential things into Simone's guest room the day I arrived at her house. Afterwards, I didn't leave my bed for two weeks. It felt as if I were in a coma. Nothing mattered but my inner thoughts that continued to taunt and torment me. Regret lay heavy on my soul, and I found myself wishing none of this had happened, wishing I could just erase the previous eight months of my life. My world as I knew it had come to a standstill, and was slowly sinking in a deep hole of depression.

I tried calling Todd numerous times – home, office, cell. He would not pick up my calls. I could only wonder how things would have ended up had I only told him. I never should have given Alana the chance. I felt so stupid. Why did I believe her? Why did I let her control when or what I would tell my man ? I wanted to rewind time, back to that moment when Todd proposed to me – I could have come clean and dealt with the consequences then and not let it turn out the way it did. At least I would have been the one to confess, I would have looked like I had a conscience, but as it stood now, I had none.

Simone entered my room with a plate of food, but I couldn't stomach anything. I was quickly losing weight and slowly losing my mind.

"How are you doing?" Simone asked as she sat down on the edge of my bed. I could only imagine how I looked, even smelled. But Simone never addressed my physical state of being; she was just concerned about helping me move past this.

"I don't want to lose him," I sighed. "I can't." I let out an emotional gasp and tears flowed down my face.

Simone slowly straightened herself on the edge of my bed. "And you won't."

"I made a huge mistake and I have no idea what to do," I said as I sat up and leaned against the headboard. "I feel so helpless, so lost right now."

"You have to talk to him," Simone said.

"He won't take my calls," I replied.

"Then keep calling him," she said, "and call from my phone if you have to, and if he still doesn't pick up, go over there."

Simone edged closer to me, crossed her legs Indian-style on the bed, and took my hands in hers. "Kai, listen to me. If you really think in your heart that this is your husband, your soulmate, then you cannot give up this easily. You have to fight for what is yours. Now I'm not saying it's going to be easy because it's not," she continued. "It's going to be damn hard, but that shouldn't stop you. If you two are really meant to be together then he will find a way to forgive you."

"What about Alana?" I wondered aloud. "What if she is still in his life, feeding him lies?"

"Then you keep feeding him the truth."

"Easier said than done."

"Listen," Simone said, "if you don't try, you'll never know"

"I know."

Simone was only saying what I knew was true in my heart, I had to get up and brush myself off. I couldn't let things end that way.

Simone turned to leave as I leaned my head back on the headboard to think. My cellphone's ring startled me and I saw a number I didn't recognize.

It was Raymond. He was calling from rehab.

•

I was finally out of the house and it felt good. The crisp air on a spring day in Chicago did wonders. I headed down to 55th and State where Raymond had been in his rehab program now for two weeks.

I entered the rehab center and waited for Raymond in their cafeteria. I was a little nervous about seeing my brother for the first time since he hit rock bottom. I pulled out my cell and scanned through my old texts. Since I didn't talk to Alana or Todd anymore, my text messaging had dropped to an all-time low. It occurred to me that I should probably just get rid of my unlimited texting altogether.

I looked up to see Raymond walking through the double glass doors. He looked healthier than I had ever seen him, but more importantly, he looked happy.

"Hey, sis," Raymond said as he took a seat next to me. I threw my arms around my brother's frail body and held him tight.

"It's good to see you, too, sis."

"How are you doing?" I asked, still looking him over.

"I'm good," he said. "The hard part is over. Two weeks of detoxing and now it's time to build myself back up."

"Two weeks of detoxing" rang in my head. I too had been through a painful detox and now I was ready for rehab, as well.

"I think this is it for me, sis," Raymond continued. "I don't want to let you or mom down."

"And I know you won't," I said, "but you just have to take one day at a time and when things get tough, just remember we are all here for you."

"I'm gonna get me a good job when I get out of here, maybe even go back to school," Raymond said. I could hear the enthusiasm for life in his voice.

"You should do whatever you want, Raymond, do what makes you happy. That's all that matters, right?"

"So how are you sis?" he asked. "How's Todd?"

Raymond's inquiry about Todd rang hard in my head, and I felt my body tensing up. I wasn't used to my drug addict brother asking about my life in any way that made me feel vulnerable and show him that I had problems too. In his eyes I was perfect, I had it together.

"We um, we're doing well," I said, hoping Raymond didn't see right through my lie. I wanted to tell him the truth, but on the real, I wasn't ready to reveal that side of my life. In my mind I felt that, if I didn't speak it aloud, somehow it wasn't true. At that point, I just wasn't ready for the split to be final.

"Todd's a good brother, sis, and you're lucky to have him in your life. There aren't too many of them left out there."

"Yeah, I know."

Hearing Raymond's words only made me hate my whole existence, made me hate the choices I'd made and the chances I'd taken. I wanted Todd back so badly.

"Are you sure you're okay, sis?" Raymond asked as he looked deep in my eyes.

"I'm good, really," I said. Talking to a sober Raymond was an unfamiliar experience for me. I had to work harder at hiding my true self from him, but it also felt good that he was one hundred percent "there" – I'd always missed that about him.

"So this program is making me examine a lot of my past, things that I need to get off my chest, you know?" Raymond was silent as he looked down then back up. "Things that I feel real bad about you know?"

"You wanna talk about it?" I said.

"I done a lot of bad things in my life, sis and… well, I feel real bad about it."

"We all do bad things, but God forgives us if we repent. He loves us regardless," I said trying to reassure my brother.

Raymond was still quiet.

"Are you okay, Raymond? What's on your mind?"

"Just, um…" Raymond looked down then back up at me. "Just this program and working to get better. Did I tell you that they gave me a part time job in here? Now I can make a little money, so when I leave I will have a little bit in my pocket."

"That's good Raymond, I'm so happy for you." I said. Although I knew there was something on my brother's chest, but it was obvious he was not ready to share it with me.

Raymond and I continued to talk for what seemed like hours. I found comfort in his voice. He had so much to share and expressed it with so much hope and excitement that I cherished every minute. I just sat there and let him sing about life and how he wanted to make big changes. The time flew by and the next thing I knew the counselor was signaling that our visit was over.

"I better go, sis, get back to the program.

Raymond looked down at the ground, then back up again at me. It was all too obvious he had something on his mind.

"Are you sure you're okay, Raymond?"

"I um," he took a deep breath. "I um, just have a lot going on right now, that's all."

"I understand, but know that I am always here to talk," I said.

Raymond leaned in and hugged me as I felt his frail body once again.

"So when you get out of here I gotta fix you a serious dinner to put some meat back on these bones of yours," I said as tears began forming in my eyes.

"Thank's, sis," Raymond said. "You know I do like to eat."

As Raymond turned to walk back through the double doors of the rehab center, my tears found their way down my face. But this time they were tears of happiness, for my brother was finally breaking free of the demons that had kept him prisoner for so many years. As I headed out of the building and down the street, I felt a small sense of renewal, a feeling that everything would be okay.

I arrived back at Simone's but decided not to crawl back into bed, but to finally make a plan to move on with my life. It was time to take action.

39 · THE REVELATION

IT HAD BEEN TWO weeks since the Alana Incident with Todd and I knew it was time to talk to him, time to stop wondering "what if," time to put my ego aside and just do it. So I picked up my cell phone, dialed Todd's number, and hit *67 to block my number from his caller ID display. I listened as the phone range a total of four times. I damn near dropped the phone when I heard Alana's voice on the other end. I quickly hung up.

I was not expecting that, not expecting Alana to answer, not expecting it at all. The mere sound of her voice knocked the wind out of me. I had to stop and sit down. Not only did I lose my fiancé, he was now hanging out with the woman I cheated with. I knew Alana and Todd were friends – okay, best friends – but how could he not be just as mad at her as he was at me? Why was he banishing me and forgiving her? My anger slowly turned to rage and I knew I couldn't leave the situation like it was. No; I had to do something, and right away.

I decided to head to my office to dig up something, anything to prove Alana wrong, to show that I was not to blame, not the initiator. I accepted that I had to take some responsibility in the matter but taking all of the blame as the person who orchestrated the whole ordeal just didn't fly with me.

I arrived at my office a few hours later and spent most of the day playing Inspector Gadget, working overtime trying to find something that I could present to Todd, anything to prove to him that I did not initiate the affair. I thought about everything from old recorded phone calls to written letters, but nothing in those would've shown that Alana was the one who orchestrated the whole thing. I felt trapped, helpless, and pissed off.

My head began to pound as I kept thinking about the conversation Alana and I had the morning after we slept together for the first time. I remembered how adamant she was about not telling Todd, how she suggested we make a pact – yeah, so much for that fucking "secret" pact. I began to realize that maybe Alana didn't have feelings for me at all; maybe she had been out to get Todd for herself the whole time.

I continued to look for evidence to prove my so-called innocence in this matter. I was down to my last straw when my assistant, Angela, dropped my cell phone bill on my desk – and, finally, for the very first time that day, I had a reasonably good idea.

"Angela, do you know if the phone company keeps a record of my texts from my cell phone?" I asked.

"I don't think so, but I have a record of them," Angela said.

I couldn't believe what I'd just heard. "You do?"

"Yeah, I synched your phone to my computer to keep a record of your texts and a few other things, just for backup."

"When did you start doing this?" I asked.

"A few weeks after I started working for you," she said. "My last boss was very forgetful so instead of arguing about what he said or didn't say, I just kept a record of it. I'm not saying that you have a bad memory or anything."

"No, I didn't think that," I replied, "but when did you have time to do all this?"

"Oh, when you were in the staff meeting every Monday morning."

At that moment I wanted to kiss my assistant. How great was that? All my text messages safely on her computer! I knew there was a reason I hired this girl, I thought. Efficiency – I loved it!

"Why didn't you ever tell me this?" I asked.

"It's more a precaution than anything," Angela said. "You're not upset, are you?"

I wanted to tell her that "upset" was the farthest thing from my mind. I was ecstatic. "No, no, not at all. As a matter of fact, you're getting a raise."

"Really?" she gasped.

"Yes," I assured her, "but let's talk about that later. Right now, can you print out some of my texts for me?"

"Sure, which ones?"

I quickly pulled out my calendar and found where I'd started my ongoing texts with Alana. I pinpointed dates ranging over eight months, wrote them down, and handed the list to my assistant.

Then a thought crossed my mind. Had Angela read them? My hunch was that she had, but I couldn't worry about that detail right then. I just needed to get those texts between Alana and me. I needed to show Todd the truth.

Angela took the paper as she gave me a look that said, "Your secret is safe with me." I smiled, thanking her for being so discreet.

Twenty minutes later I had all the texts between Alana and me in my hand. I quickly read over them just to make sure the evidence was what I needed. Once I saw that I could definitely show Todd the truth, I grabbed my things, headed out of my office, and drove straight to his house.

40 · PUT UP OR SHUT UP

I SAT IN FRONT of Todd's house, contemplating what I would say to him, wondering if he would even believe what came out of my mouth. But he had to. I had proof, written proof, that Alana was the one who started this whole affair, not me. I took a deep breath and headed toward his building. I approached the door, punched in the security code that I had memorized, and the front door opened. I headed into the lobby.

I was starting to get very nervous and I felt small droplets of sweat forming on my nose and forehead with each step that I took. I wanted to turn around, but I continued to walk down the corridor until I saw Todd's door – our door. I stopped in front of it and double-checked to make sure I had the proof in my purse, then rang the doorbell. I heard footsteps heading my way and my throat became instantly dry, so I swallowed hard, trying to keep my voice from cracking. I thought about jetting down the hallway before it was too late, but before I was able to make my great escape, or even think much more about it, Todd opened the door. He just stood there. The look of discontent on his face paralyzed my thoughts and disabled my game plan.

"What are you doing here?" he asked.

I cleared my throat, hoping my voice wouldn't shake, quiver, or crack. "I um, I need to talk to you."

"Kai, there's nothing to talk about," Todd said. He tried to close the door but I stopped him.

"Please, just five minutes," I pleaded.

Then I heard that familiar voice in the background.

"Who's at the door?" Alana asked as she appeared behind Todd.

"What is going on Todd? Why is she here?" I asked.

"Why am I here? I don't think that's any business of yours," Alana said.

"If you haven't forgotten, she was in this with me, you know the familiar saying – it takes two to tangle," I said, trying to get Todd to wake the fuck up and see that Alana was just as guilty, if not more.

"But you cheated," Alana said as she stepped forward.

"And you deceived your best friend. Todd, don't you see that?" I asked.

"Kai, just go," Todd said.

As Todd tried to close the door again, I remembered what Simone said, that it wasn't going to be easy, so I had to keep trying. I stuck my foot in the door before Todd had a chance to close it. "Can I please just talk to you, alone? All I'm asking for is five minutes."

Todd just stared at me, then said, "Whatever you need to say, Kai, just say it."

I stood there, wishing that Alana were not in our space, in our moment, and thinking that maybe I should come back when she wasn't around. But then again, she needed to hear the real truth just like Todd.

"Can I at least come in?"

"Fine."

Todd stepped aside as Alana rolled her eyes, grunted, and headed to the living room. I closed the front door behind me and followed them in.

"So what's up?" Todd began as he sat down next to Alana on the couch.

"I can't believe you're hanging out with her," I said, unable to control my feelings.

"She came to me with the truth, which is more than I can say for you," Todd said.

"Actually, Todd, she didn't tell you the truth. I have proof that Alana initiated this whole affair."

"Proof how?" Alana said.

I pulled out the 15 pages of text messages between Alana and me, with the incriminating ones highlighted, proving that Alana had been the initiator, proving that she was a big fat liar. I handed them to Todd. I took a step back as Todd read over what I hoped would show him that his so-called best friend was twisted.

The room fell silent as Todd stared at the papers in his hands. I watched as his right temple began to pulsate. I shot Alana a look as she seethed at me, looking ready to attack.

Todd slowly looked up from the papers, looked at Alana, then finally turned to me.

"How did you get this?" Todd asked.

"My assistant synced all the incoming and outgoing text messages from my cell phone to her computer."

"You can't do that," Alana said.

"Yeah, you can. It's called technology, Alana, you might want to learn about it."

"Shut up!" Alana hissed.

"You shut up!" I said.

"Why don't you make me shut up!" she retorted.

"I'm right here," I said.

"How about you both shut the fuck up!" Todd yelled.

Todd directed his attention back to the messages in his hand. Alana stood up and tried to grab them, but Todd jerked his arm away and continued to read them as he walked to the other side of the living room. Todd slowly lowered the paper and turned to Alana.

"So you initiated this shit?"

"Hell, no, she is obviously lying," Alana shot back.

Todd stared at the papers that he clutched in his hand.

Alana knew she was busted, but like a rat trapped in a corner, she was going to come out fighting.

"Todd," Alana said, breaking silence, "for all we know her twisted ass could have typed up all of these messages and now she's trying to pass them off as the truth."

"Nice try, Alana, but no," I said.

"Why don't you just stay out of this?" Alana demanded.

"Oh, I am so all over this, Alana," I continued. I had come this far and was not about to be quiet. This shit ain't over until the dejected bitch sings, I said to myself.

Todd continued riffling through the papers, then looked back at Alana.

"You made me believe that Kai orchestrated this whole thing, that you were just an innocent bystander."

"I was," Alana said in her most convincing tone.

"Please," I told Todd, "just take Alana's story and reverse it. Everything Alana told you I did, she was the one who actually did it."

"This is some bullshit. I didn't lie," Alana said.

"Yes you did, just like you're lying right now," I said.

"Shut up!" Alana snapped as she tried reaching for the papers one last time, but Todd managed to keep them away from her. "Todd, I don't know why you would believe Kai anyway. I mean, come on, she cheated on you."

"Are these your texts, Alana?" Todd asked.

Alana shook her head in disbelief. She was trying her best to keep her lies going. "Todd, I can't even believe you're taking her side. I've known you for fifteen years."

"No one is taking sides Alana, I'm just trying to get to the bottom of this fucked up shit." Todd took a deep breath and began to pace the room. I felt I needed to say something, anything, to seal my deal.

"Well, here's the bottom line, Todd," I began. "I was going to tell you but Alana made me swear not to, claiming you would never understand. Then the moment we got engaged she decided to come clean." I glared at Alana. "She was jealous that we were getting married."

"Oh, give me a fucking break, Kai, you never meant to tell Todd," Alana said. "If so, you wouldn't have let it go on for as long as it did." She turned to Todd, then said, "Honestly, I think Kai liked fucking me more than she liked fucking you."

"Oh please, it wasn't about who I liked fucking better," I said. "I made a mistake and the biggest mistake was keeping it from you, Todd. I was curious and I let curiosity get the best of me, but it's over now and I promise to never hurt you like that again."

Although that sounded great, it wasn't 100 percent true, since I did still have feelings for Alana. But the more she revealed her true self the more I realized that those feelings were fading, and fast.

Todd was silent, but for the first time since we had broken up he gave me a look that told me he still cared.

"Do you believe me?" I asked, making sure that what I had said had sunk in.

Todd rubbed his head, then his face. "I don't know what to believe anymore. One thing I do know for sure is that you two hooked up, but the question is who initiated this shit."

I couldn't believe what I was hearing; Todd's anger didn't come from me cheating on him with Alana, but from the thought of me initiating it.

"I know what I did was wrong," I said firmly, "but I still love you."

Todd and I held a stare before he looked back down at the papers he held in his hands.

"You have got to be fucking kidding me! You are actually taking her side, you fucking bastard!" Alana yelled.

"I'm not taking anyone's side, I'm just trying to figure out what the hell went down!" Todd yelled back.

"I can tell you what went down," Alana replied, "that bitch is crazy."

"Alana, will you just shut the fuck up so I can think?" Todd shot back. Todd began to pace again. Then he stopped and looked at the both of us. "Actually, I just need you two to leave."

"What?" Alana asked.

"Just get out," Todd repeated.

"Why should I leave? She should be the one leaving, not me," Alana said.

"No, I need both of you to leave so I can think this through," Todd said, "and right now, you two are driving me crazy."

"I agree. I think we both should leave," I said, echoing Todd's wishes.

"Thank you, Kai," Todd said with a sigh of relief.

"I do love you, Todd," I said, determined to throw that in before making my exit.

"This is ridiculous. Would you please get 'd' over it," Alana exclaimed.

"How is this so ridiculous, Alana?" I asked.

"Because Todd doesn't love you, Kai. If he did he would have told you the truth by now."

"Alana!" Todd barked.

"What – what truth?" I asked haltingly.

"The secret. Our secret," Alana said.

"Alana, don't!" Todd shouted.

"No, Todd, I think it's time for Kai to know that little secret of yours – or should I say 'ours'?"

In that moment, I felt like an outsider. They had a secret that I knew nothing of.

"What the hell are you talking about?" I demanded, wanting to know, but not wanting to know at the same.

"Well, Kai," Alana said, "Riley is actually Todd's daughter."

"You're lying," I said.

"No, actually, this time I'm not. Tell her Todd."

Todd was silent, and stood very still as if contemplating what to say next.

Alana smiled a smug, self-satisfied smile. "Well, the secret is out, or as you like to say, Kai, the cat is out the fuckin' bag."

Alana directed her attention to Todd. "Tell her, Todd, tell Kai how once upon a time we were more than just platonic friends and Riley is the result of that."

At that point I didn't know who or what to believe, especially when it came out of Alana's mouth. So I turned to Todd and looked him directly in his eyes.

"Todd, is that true?" I asked.

Todd and I held a stare a very long stare. His eyes were filled with remorse and guilt and I knew the answer before he even uttered one word.

"Yes, but it happened before I even met you and –"

"What?" It felt like I was sucker-punched me in the gut.

"I was going to tell you before we got married," he said.

"But the fact is, Todd, ya didn't," Alana said, finishing Todd's sentence.

"I can't believe this," I protested. "I asked you, I asked you if you had been with her."

"Kai, it's not what you think," Todd said.

"I think it is, and more," Alana said with a smirk.

Alana picked up her things, preparing for her exit, but quickly turned back around. "By the way, I'm sure it's pretty hard for you to hear all this since, well –" Alana gave me a cold, hard look. "You know, since you can't have kids of your own."

"What – what did you say?" I asked, not believing what I had just heard.

Oh, Todd told me all about how you were raped as a child and contracted Chlamydia, and because you never got it treated you're now sterile," Alana looked at Todd. "Isn't that what you told me, Todd, did I leave anything out?"

Todd just stood there, silently seething as he stared back at Alana.

"Pity," Alana said.

"Why are you doing this?" Todd screamed.

"Because you don't have the balls to," Alana shot back.

As Alana and Todd's argument escalated, my heart began to pound. The horrors of my past flashed before my eyes, pulling me into a place that was so dark I felt my body losing control. The next thing I knew I was on top of Alana, slamming my fist into that face I once called beautiful. I felt nothing but rage and I released every bit of it out on her. Everything seemed to be moving in slow motion, everything but my mind, which was racing out of control.

Todd pulled me off of Alana, who was screaming as blood flowed from her nose and covered her face, neck, and shirt.

I struggled to get out of Todd's grip. I was out of breath and sweating profusely. I backed up, slowly taking in the events of the night and what I had just done. Surveying the scene, I struggled to wrap my mind around what had just happened. I looked up to see Alana screaming out of control and Todd just staring at me. I couldn't say a word.

Without thinking, I grabbed my belonging and ran out of the door. I was shaking violently. I felt like throwing up. Never in a million years did I think my confrontation would end like that, not with my deepest secret being revealed, not with me losing my fucking mind, and for damn sure not with Todd being the father of Alana's child. I jumped in my car and just drove, not knowing where I was going or what I was going to do next.

41 · SISTER ACT

THE NEXT FEW DAYS I was in a daze. I couldn't believe that what I was actually experiencing was my life, my truth, my reality. Less than eight months before I was happy, content, and living a normal existence. I wanted to wake up and breathe a sigh of relief from the horrible nightmare I was having. But I couldn't. It wasn't a dream, it was my life.

I tossed and turned in my bed in Simone's guest room. I was unable to sleep. My mind kept racing and would not stop. My fears and regrets tormented me – telling me how I shouldn't have done what I did, wishing I could turn back time and undo it all. I was going insane, and I needed to make all this go away. But it wouldn't. It just kept replaying in my mind, over and over again.

I finally found the strength to head down to the kitchen and get something to eat. I wasn't hungry but I knew I needed to eat. I opened the refrigerator to find a plate of food with a note from Simone: "Just heat and serve." I smiled and thanked God for keeping her in my life.

I made myself eat about a third of what was on the plate and tossed the rest. My stomach ached with each bite as if I were swallowing tiny teaspoons of poison. Hours seemed like minutes as my mind drifted back to everything that had brought me to my present-day nightmare. I had no one to blame but myself; I created this life that held me prisoner, and I was the only one who had the key to freedom.

A knock at the door startled me, and for the moment brought me out of my deep, dark trance. I was hesitant to open the door. I wasn't ready to face anyone in the outside world; I was comfortable in my cave, alone, isolated, and depressed.

The person was persistent, making me feel like I had no choice but to face whomever was on the other side of that door. I opened it. To my dismay it was Mila. She stood before me as we stared intensely at one another. I wasn't prepared for her; not Mila, not now.

"Mila, if you're here to rub all this in my face, I can't do that right now."

"That's not why I'm here," Mila said in a soft, unthreatening voice. I then noticed tears in her eyes and a look of forgiveness on her face. She stepped forward and embraced me lovingly and completely. I could feel the soft heat of her breath on my neck as she exhaled. As I embraced Mila, I couldn't remember the last time I'd ever seen my sister cry – maybe as a child, but not as an adult. Mila began to speak but her emotions got the best of her and she started sobbing muffled words instead. I held her, feeling weak, but not wanting to let her go. We finally parted and she looked deep into my eyes.

"I am so sorry, Kai, for the way that I've treated you all our lives. I don't blame you for hating me, because, well, I hate myself," Mila said as she spoke between sniffles in a soft, gentle tone. I couldn't believe the amount of emotion that was pouring from my sister.

"Mila –" I began.

"No, let me finish," she said. "I was always very jealous of you. You were such a free spirit even when we were told not to be. You did what made you feel good. On the other hand, I lived my life safe, always worried about what someone was going to think, and because of that I was miserable. I married a man who loved his job more than me and I acted like it was okay. But not any more. I can't live another day like this."

I stood there as Mila unloaded her heavy heart to me. I stared at Mila, but felt like I was seeing a totally different person, a person with a heart. "Wow, this is a whole lot, Mila," I said, trying to think of something to add, but absolutely nothing came to mind.

"I know I'm dumping a lot on you right now, Kai, but you really opened my eyes the other night and, and you are right, about everything."

Mila was blowing my mind, but I had to admit, it felt good to hear her say these words. The night I'd stormed out of her house, I had no idea what would come of our relationship. We'd had our fights in the past but nothing, I mean nothing, compared to the last one.

Mila dropped her head, took a deep breath, and said, "I think my marriage is over."

Truth be told, Mila's marriage was over on her wedding day. But given Mila's outpour of honesty, discretion prevailed and I bit my tongue. I was just glad that she finally was able to see it for herself.

"I'm sorry, Mila. Is there anything I can do?"

"Just be here for me, if you can. I know you have your own life and issues."

"Yeah, but we can be there for each other," I said.

"Thanks," Mila said.

"So have you asked Charles for a divorce yet?"

"Not yet. First I'm going to ask him to go to counseling and if he won't, then I'll ask him for a divorce. If he is not willing to work on our marriage, then what sense does it make to stay? I'm tired of being miserable, Kai. I want to be happy."

I couldn't believe what I was hearing; my sister was actually owning up to her feelings, her real feelings. She was no longer acting like they didn't exist, or pretending they didn't matter. And that, right there, was the beginning of Mila reclaiming her life, the life she was always meant to live.

My reunion with Mila was so overwhelming I didn't see the small Asian man standing behind her in the hallway. I didn't even realize that we were still standing partway in the hall. I stepped aside and he stepped closer to me.

"You Kai Edwards?" he asked with a thick accent.

"Yes, I am," I said.

He handed me a small envelope. "You've just been served. Good day."

I stared at the envelope, not really registering what was happening until Mila spoke. "Kai, who's suing you?"

"I, I don't know," I said slowly as I opened the envelope.

It was Alana. She was suing me for assault and battery.

"What the hell," I said, reading the summons to myself before sharing it with Mila. "Alana is suing me for wages lost due to a broken nose and her inability to work as a model," I said as I slowly walked into the house and sat down. Mila closed the door behind us and followed me back into the kitchen.

"Oh, my God, what? Why? What happened?" Mila asked.

I told Mila everything and spared no details. Mila told me that Alana deserved much more than a broken nose. She even volunteered to go over there and break her nose again, but I told Mila that wasn't necessary. But I had to laugh, imagining Mila fighting, Miss Priss herself, but then again she seemed to be full of surprises.

"I wanna go with you to court," Mila said.

"Thanks, but I need to do this alone. It's my mess and I need to sort it out, by myself."

"Well, I want to do something to help, all right?" Mila asked.

Then I had a thought. I looked at her and said, "Go see Raymond, then. It would mean a lot to him – and me."

Mila looked at me. "Okay, I guess it's the least I could do for being such a bitch most of my life."

"Most?" I asked jokingly.

Mila shot me a mean look then laughed out loud. I laughed right along with her. Mila ended up staying the rest of the day, as we rekindled a friendship and a sisterhood that was long dormant. It was a nice distraction with the Alana mess hanging over my head. I was enjoying a reunion with a long-lost soul, because that day I met a woman named Mila Edwards – someone I would be proud to call my twin sister.

42 · FORGIVENESS

THE MORNING OF THE court hearing I woke up nauseated. I couldn't hold anything down and I wasn't even sure at first if I was going to make it. By noon I felt okay as my nerves slowly subsided. I think subconsciously I was looking for a way out, a reason not to go, but I knew I had no choice; I had to face the music, even if I hated the song. Simone was in her back office as I headed to the kitchen. I heard her on the phone as I grabbed some coffee she'd made and sipped on it slowly. Simone came into the kitchen and set a piece of paper with a number on it in front of me.

"My lawyer is going to meet you at the courthouse this morning."

"Simone," I said, "I told you I didn't need a lawyer."

"Really? And how many years of law school have you completed again? Oh, right, none," Simone said.

I stared at the number in front of me as Simone sat down in the chair across from me.

"Listen, Kai," she said, "don't be naïve and most of all don't be unprepared. Alana provoked you. She is an instigator, a manipulator, and a bitch. Besides, as good as my lawyer is, by the time you walk out that courtroom, the judge will be thinking she attacked you."

I took a deep breath. My stomach started feeling nauseous again. My nerves were marching toward the pit of my stomach with a vengeance.

"Thanks," I said as I took the number and slid it in my pocket. I grabbed my coat to leave, and Simone followed suit.

"What are you doing?"

"Oh, I'm going with you," she said.

"Simone!"

"I'm going with you, Kai," Simone said again, this time with a firm tone.

I gave her a reassuring smile, then we headed out of the door.

Although I tried to act brave and independent, I was relieved that Simone was going to be at my side, because on the real, I was scared as hell.

•

We waited outside the courtroom for the case to be called. I was nervous and anxious all rolled up in one. I didn't know what to expect nor did I know how to mentally prepare for this moment. But when Alana entered the courthouse with her nose bandaged up, I quickly realized that I should be expecting a lot. I couldn't stop staring at her. She looked worse than I remembered, almost as if she were trying way too hard.

Alana and I made eye contact and she gave me a self-satisfied grin. I looked away, but Simone quickly flashed her the finger accompanied with a polite smile, then leaned over towards me.

"Don't let her bother you," Simone whispered. "She is just

trying to mess with you. Her nose probably isn't even broken, dramatic bitch."

"Yeah, but I did hit her pretty hard," I replied. "God, I can't believe I snapped like that." I started to feel hot, my hands got all clammy, and my throat started to close up.

"You may have snapped, but she provoked you by revealing something in your past that is a trigger point for you," Simone continued, "so if you ask me, she had the shit coming."

Simone glanced over at Alana, then back at me. "See, it's all fun and games until someone ends up in triage," Simone said in her reassuring voice.

I smiled, probably for the first time that morning. I loved my friend Simone.

"Are you sure this lawyer is a good as you say he is?"

"Better," Simone responded.

I took a deep breath, took one more glance over at Alana's direction, then turned back to Simone.

"Can you get me some water?" I asked.

"Be right back."

As Simone headed down the hallway to retrieve a cup of water for me, I laid my head back against the wall and closed my eyes. I tried to visualize everything going smoothly and in my favor, but each time I tried to fill my mind with a positive thought, a negative one would come and steal it away. It was a constant battle and it was making me crazy. My head was spinning, so much that I didn't notice anyone standing in front of me until I heard a familiar voice.

"Hey." The deep voice startled me as I opened my eyes to see Todd standing over me. He was dressed in a beige suit, white shirt, and blue tie. He looked very handsome, but then again he always looked handsome to me.

"What are you doing here?" I asked as I slowly stood.

"Support."

"For who? Me or Alana?" I asked.

I stared at Todd and even though I was hurt by what he

had done, the pain always seemed to burn less when I factored in what I had added to the mix. Truth be told, we were both at fault, although we were both human too. But that doesn't take away the pain, the hurt, or the guilt.

"For both of you."

"Right, of course," I said.

"So who's representing you?" he continued

"It's actually Simone's lawyer, Patrick O'Neal, have you heard of him?"

"Yeah, he's good."

"Well, I hope so," I said.

"You look nice," Todd said.

"Thanks."

Todd and I stood there for a minute without words. There was so much I wanted to say to him but at the same time I felt numb. I couldn't believe how all this had turned out, how we'd ended up here. I turned to see Simone standing with Patrick who had just arrived. She gestured for me to come and join them.

"I'd better go," I said.

"Yeah, of course," Todd said.

I gave Todd one last look then headed over to Simone and Patrick to go into the courtroom.

Exactly one hour and twenty minutes later, after hearing all the evidence, which also included one very bizarre story, the judge ended up throwing out the case. I guess he figured Alana had it coming. But he did reprimand me about striking back in violence, so I quickly apologized and promised that it would never happen again.

I wanted to laugh, thinking that because of me Alana will probably finagle a way to get a nose job out of this in hopes to further her career even more.

Simone and I headed out the courtroom, and as I passed Alana we locked eyes. Her stare was emotionless. I quickly looked away but I had to wonder how my life would've been if

I had never explored with her. Regardless, I was ready to put all of it behind me and it was the perfect time.

I looked for Todd but he was nowhere to be found. I was not sure if he'd stayed for the whole hearing or not, but at that moment, I didn't much care. I headed outside the courthouse and for the first time, I felt free, free from lies, free from deceit, free from a prison that I'd managed to create for myself.

It was time to start over.

43 · WHAT LIES AHEAD

IT HAD BEEN A month since my court fiasco with Alana and I was finally settling back into work mode. My thoughts often drifted to Todd and Alana. I wondered if they were still together as friends or maybe as lovers. I knew Todd was pretty mad at her, but crazier things have happened and I wouldn't be totally surprised if Alana finally wore him down. I mean, hell, they do have a child together, so why wouldn't he just be with her?

I continued to work overtime to push any thoughts of them out of my mind, but I couldn't. Those thoughts had a way of creeping in at any opportunity.

I was quickly pulled out of my daily Todd/Alana trance when Simone slid a piece of paper in front of me. I took my focus off my thoughts as I glanced down to see a name and a number.

"What is this?" I said.

"The job in New York, it's yours if you want it," Simone said as she walked over to my couch and sat down. I got up from my desk to join her. Ever since things went south with Todd and Alana, I had been toying with the idea of moving out of Chicago. I hadn't talked to Todd since my court date and the thought of running into either one of them sent a chill through my body. I wondered how I would feel or even act, should that situation come up. I went so far as to mentally prepare myself for a chance meeting. I thought it was inevitable. Chicago is a giant city, but it has a way of being like a very small town when you are trying to avoid people, particularly your ex- boyfriend and his best friend/my ex-female lover,/her baby's daddy.

I glanced back down at the name and number on the yellow Post-It. I knew this was something I should pursue. It felt right.

"This is the opening at Benton Advertising?" I asked.

"Yep, it's an amazing opportunity. I already talked to the executive director, so you just have to make that phone call."

I guess Simone realized, just as much as I did that staying in Chicago right then was not only hindering my work productivity, but morphing me into a hermit. In the previous two months I had managed to find ways to occupy myself within the parameters that I like to call "my condo," and although decorating had never been my forte, I managed to revamp my entire place from floor to ceiling.

I took a deep breath, contemplating what I should do, weighing my options in my head. "You really think I should take this job, huh?"

"Very much so. Kai don't take this the wrong way, but you've become pretty fucking boring."

"Thanks," I said. "So tell me how you really feel, Simone."

"Listen," she continued, "I know you've been through a shit load of crap, but the truth is I can't keep you focused on your work to save both of our lives, not to mention our jobs."

"So you're firing me?"

"Of course not," she said. "I'm simply taking a big distraction out of your life."

"I'll still be thinking about this big distraction in New York," I sighed.

"Of course you will, but the difference is, you won't have that fear hovering over you of running into either of them and that is what's really weighing you down."

Simone was right, I was letting this situation with Alana and Todd dictate how I lived, and where I went in the city, and that was not healthy at all.

"Besides, you always said you wanted to move to New York," Simone said, "so here's your chance, right?"

"I guess you're right."

"Of course I'm right, momma's always right."

I smiled at Simone's confident response as she jumped up from my couch and checked her watch.

"I'm going to grab some lunch," she said. "You wanna come?"

"No, I actually brought mine," I said, realizing how I must have sounded.

"You know, Kai, time doesn't stop just because you are afraid to venture out into the world. Don't be that person that looks up and realizes your life is half over and you should've done this or should've done that. Life is too damn short for that."

"I know, I know," I said.

"Well, then, prove me wrong. Call that number."

"I will."

Simone stopped and gave me an endearing look. "I will miss the hell out of you."

"Ditto," I said.

"Ciao bella, baby."

Simone left. I continued to stare at the phone number sitting on my desk when my cell phone rang. I didn't expect nor could explain the message that flashed across my screen. That's because it was from Todd and he wanted to see me; he needed to talk about something. I stared at the text message, wondering what he wanted to talk about. I continued to read the message a few more times, before setting down my phone to contemplate my next move. Should I go, should I ignore it, should I text him back declining the offer? I felt butterflies multiplying in my stomach. I could feel my heartbeat speeding up, then slowing down. The timing couldn't have been more perfect and yet more unexpected at the same time. I quickly picked my phone back up and typed, "How does 1pm sound?"

•

I was running late to meet Todd for the simple reason that I couldn't stop critiquing myself in the mirror before I headed out the office. I was excited to see him and, although I had no idea what would come of our meeting, it would be good to finally talk.

I jumped out of the cab and headed toward the restaurant. I was nervous and anxious at the same time. I couldn't imagine what he wanted to talk about or why. I was imagining what I would say, how I would act. I entered the restaurant and immediately spotted Todd; he gestured to me as I slowly walked toward the back of the room. My throat was dry and I couldn't feel the hard, Spanish stone tiles under my feet as they carried me closer to him. I approached the table as Todd stood, leaned over, and gently kissed me on the check.

"You look good," Todd said as he slowly sat back down on his chair.

"Thanks," I said as I took a seat across from him.

"How are you?" Todd asked.

"I'm good, and you?" I replied.

"I um, I can't complain," Todd said as he cleared his throat then took a sip of his ice water sitting in front of him.

We were both uncomfortable and for very good reasons. I didn't know what to say, where to start, or how to say it. But before I knew it I was blurting out the first thing that popped in my head, which is not always the best course of action.

"So are you two a couple now?" I asked. I immediately regretted it.

Todd stared at me, before clearing his throat once again and taking yet another a sip of water. "Who?"

"Who else, you and Alana," I said.

Todd chuckled, looking down then back up.

I didn't understand what brought on the chuckle. I mean, they did have a fucking child together. I was starting to get myself all worked up again; I had to take a deep calming breath before continuing. "Well, I just figured since you two have a child together –"

Todd just stared at me. "Actually, Kai, that's one of the reasons I wanted to talk to you, to explain."

"Explain what?" I asked. "How you lied and told me you were never with her?"

Todd adjusted himself in his seat. "I really don't think you have the right to point any fingers in this situation," he shot back.

"Right, sorry," I said, as I fell silent. The brother had a valid point.

"Listen, Kai, what happened between Alana and me was a one-time thing, and it was way before I ever met you. Alana and I never dated or even thought about having a relationship."

I wanted to say, "I beg to differ" for Alana's sake.

"But," he continued, "we did have that one night together and as a result of that, well, she got pregnant with Riley."

"Are you 100 percent sure she's yours? I mean, I wouldn't just take Alana's word for it," I said.

"No she's mine," Todd said. "I took a paternity test."

I was silent, feeling a wave of sadness flow over me, losing hold of that one-percent hope that just maybe Riley wasn't his, that maybe it was her ex-husband's child. Then my next thought was that Alana was able to give Todd a child, at least, something I could never do.

"I see. So you're still friends?" I asked.

Todd was silent, looking as if he were searching for the right words to answer that question. He looked away, then back up, then directly into my eyes.

"Actually, Kai," he said, "Alana and I are a couple now."

I didn't know if I was more stunned, shocked, or confused.

"What? A what?" I asked. I couldn't believe what I was hearing. I mean, I feared it, suspected it, but to hear it confirmed was something that burned like a shot of Hennessey shooting down my throat. "You're a, a couple?"

"Kai, we do have a child together and well, she is my best friend."

Yeah, a best friend who will never love you the way I do, I thought. "Todd, Alana is using you, don't you see that? She uses everyone."

"She wouldn't do that to me," he said.

I couldn't believe what I was hearing. This was not the man that I'd fallen in love with – or maybe it was. Maybe I just never saw him for who he was: a fucking idiot.

"Todd, Alana is a manipulator, I mean, come on, you've seen how she's manipulated everyone who's come into her life. Hell, she had both of us on her stupid puppet strings, for Christ's sake."

"She may have had you, but not me," Todd insisted.

"Oh, really?" I asked. "Did you ever think about Alana orchestrating this whole thing between her and me, just so you could find out, making me out to be the bad guy, just so she could be with you?"

"Okay," he said, "now you're reaching, Kai"

"Todd, you saw the text messages, which proves that she's a liar, so why wouldn't you think that she is capable of more?"

"Because I've known her for too long."

"Even more of a reason," I said.

"Kai, listen," Todd said. "I understand where you are coming from, you're hurt, confused. But the bottom line, after all that has gone down, is that I think it's better this way."

"Has she drugged you? Todd, Alana is a horrible person."

"Kai, no one is a saint, okay. And just because people do horrible things doesn't always make them a horrible person."

I wasn't really sure where all of this was coming from; my only guess was that Todd had always been in love with Alana, and just chose not to admit it to himself – or to me.

"After what happened between the two of you," he said, "Alana came clean."

"Again, huh?"

"She told me everything, even the things that made her look bad."

"Oh really?" I retorted. "Did she tell you when we first started this affair, she was adamant that I never tell you about me and her, saying that you would never understand? But what she was doing was giving herself a free hand to tell you when she was ready. Don't you see what she was doing? It was all part of a master plan."

Todd stared at me. I was hoping that I was breaking through the wall of disbelief that kept him from seeing his relationship with Alana as it really was – a sham.

Todd took a sip of water, He was pretty calm and cool, and maybe because he had been thinking about this for a while, maybe he was finally seeing the light. "I can't hear anymore of this, it is just fucking crazy."

"Not as crazy as Alana," I replied.

"Why are you telling me all of this?" Todd asked.

"Because I want you to see the person you are choosing to be with."

"Why? Because I am choosing to be with her and not with you?" he asked.

"No, because you deserve much better, that's why. Are you even in love with her?"

"She's the mother of my child," Todd said.

"Well, that answers my question," I said.

"This was a bad idea," Todd said. "I'd better go." He stood to leave.

"When did you find out Riley was your child?" I asked.

Todd was silent. He looked away.

"It was the night you stood me up. The night I saw you and Alana at the restaurant together, wasn't it?"

"Yeah."

"Why didn't you just break it off with me then? Why wait?"

"Because I did love you," he answered.

"And now?"

"Now things are different and I think I need to be with the mother of my child, do the right thing."

"Does the mother of your child know you came to meet me?" I asked.

"She doesn't need to know," Todd said. "This is between you and me."

"No, see that's where you're wrong," I said. "It was never between just me and you."

"I better go," he repeated. He turned and began to walk away.

"I'm moving to New York next week," I said, catching his attention.

Todd stopped and turned back around, a flash of pain spread across his face. He tried his best to hide it. "Good luck with that, and I hope you find someone special out there."

"Yeah, me too," I said flatly.

Todd walked away. As I watched him walk through the restaurant and out the front door, leaving me alone, I couldn't help but think how Alana had a strong hold over Todd just like she once had over me. And just like me, Todd was clueless.

I headed out of the restaurant as tears flowed down my face and just then I remembered the very first day Todd and I had met at that quaint coffee shop on Wacker Drive. I remembered thinking of how I was going to spend the rest of my life with that man. I thought about how I didn't realize that one single choice could change all of that.

And it did.

44 · EXPECT THE UNEXPECTED

I STARED AT THE multitude of boxes sitting in Simone's living room, each one meticulously marked as bathroom stuff, bedroom stuff, kitchen stuff, and other stuff. I was packing up the last of my things as I waited for the movers to arrive. It was already 3:45 in the afternoon and they were officially 45 minutes late. If that was any iindication of the quality of their service, I was readying myself to log a complaint.

The past three weeks had been an emotional rollercoaster. I hadn't slept much and keeping a substantial amount of food down had been out of the question. I continued to go back and forth, wondering if I were doing the right thing by moving. I realized New York would be a fresh start, but at the same time I didn't know too many people there. I was 33 years old and had come to the harsh reality that as one grew older it became that much harder to find genuine friendships. It was not because people just grow evil as they grow older, but because as we age we gain more responsibility and with that comes less time to cultivate lasting friendships. It was one more reason to hold on to your childhood and college friends, because they are where your roots are.

I was starting to become restless with the movers still not there, so I went to call them. Just as I was about to dial the number my door buzzer went off. I headed to the door a bit annoyed, but when I opened it I realized that it was not the movers but my brother Raymond.

"Hey, sis."

Raymond stood in front of me looking like he just stepped out of an Old Navy ad. He was wearing blue faded jeans and a long sleeve t-shirt with a olive green short sleeve one pulled over it. His hair was freshly cut and surprisingly for the first time in years he didn't smell like the streets that once consumed him.

"Raymond, hey!" I said as I reached out to embrace him.

"Look at you, you look great!" I said as I scanned Raymond from head to toe, and then back up again.

"Thanks, sis, I guess I clean up well, huh?" Raymond said with a small chuckle in his voice.

"This is a surprise," I said as I stepped back to let him enter.

"Well, I got the message you left for me at the center, saying you needed to talk to me, so I figured instead of calling you I would stop by. The center lets me leave for two hours a day."

"Okay, well, I'm glad you stopped by," I said.

I realized telling Raymond that I was moving wasn't going to be easy but I knew this was something that I had to do. Raymond entered and immediately zeroed in on all of the boxes occupying Simone's 900 square-foot condo.

"What's going on, sis, whose moving?"

"I am, to New York."

"New York, why?" he asked.

"Well, I got a new job."

"When did you decide all this?"

"Well," I answered, "it was kind of sudden, but I had to act fast if I wanted it."

"Is Todd moving with you?"

I stared at Raymond, realizing that he had been in the dark about my life for a long, long time, and although I was starting to feel at peace where I was, I still wasn't ready to tell him everything, not yet.

"Todd and I aren't together anymore," I said as I took a deep breath.

"What happened? Are you okay?" Raymond asked as he slowly sat down on the chocolate brown ottoman.

"Actually, I'm fine," I said. "I just know that it is for the best."

"He didn't cheat on you did he, sis?" Raymond asked in his protective, brotherly voice.

"No, he didn't. I really don't want to get into it right now, but just know that everything is good."

Raymond stood and walked over to me and just stared at me with a look of sadness mixed with admiration.

"I know you'll be fine, sis, you're a strong woman, believe me I know. I don't think I would be standing here if it weren't for you in my life. I owe you a lot, sis," Raymond said as tears filled his eyes. "More than you know."

"Raymond, you don't owe me anything, I'm just glad I was able to be there for you. All I ask is that you stay on this path because it looks good on you, ya know?" I ran both of my hands down his arms to his hands. I took his hands into mine. "I'm very proud of you."

"Yeah, but what am I gonna do without you in Chicago?" he sniffed.

"Come on," I said, "you'll be fine. Soon you will be out of the program and back on your feet. Besides, New York isn't that far away. I can come back to visit on weekends."

Raymond smiled. "I guess you're right, but I'm going to miss the hell out of you, sis."

"Ditto," I said.

We shared a quiet moment.

"I better go," Raymond said before turning to leave, but then stopped and slowly turned back toward me. "Hey, sis, um, you still having those dreams?"

Raymond's question brought back the harsh memories that I could never seem to shake. I felt my body tense. I took a deep breath to release it. "Yeah, I am." I stared at my brother as he looked away, his eyes diverting to the floor. "Why?"

Raymond shifted from side to side as if he had something to say.

"What is it, Raymond?"

"Nothing," he said.

"Raymond, talk to me," I said as I stepped in closer to him, lifting his head so our eyes could meet.

"I did something bad, sis," Raymond said as tears filled his eyes and sorrow engulfed his face.

"What is it Raymond tell me, please," I pleaded.

"I did something very bad and you didn't deserve it, you didn't deserve what happened to you."

I touched Raymond's arm and I could feel him trembling. Something was very wrong and it was freaking the hell out of me.

"Raymond, what are you talking about? You're scaring me."

Raymond stared at me for a minute, then said, "Your dreams, I was the cause of them."

"What?" I asked.

"I made them do it," Raymond continued.

"Made who do what, Raymond, you're not making any sense," I said.

Raymond began to sob as he tried to speak. "When we were kids, I told them, I told them they could do... things with you in exchange for…a hit."

"What? What are you saying to me?" I asked, as a cold chill ripped through my body. I placed my hand on my chest, not initially wanting to believe what my brother was telling me.

"Please," he cried, "don't be mad."

"Don't be mad? You sold me out for some drugs!" I screamed, as my body began to tense as my deepest darkest memories flashed again before my eyes. I felt sick, weak, and furious. In that moment, I felt a wave of anger flow over me, something I had never felt before in my entire life.

"I'm so sorry, sis, I should have protected you," Raymond said, now crying uncontrollably, simultaneously begging for forgiveness.

"Raymond, they raped me!" I screamed.

"I didn't know," he said, "I didn't think they would take it that far. I was stupid. God, what have I done? I am so sorry. Please, please forgive me."

"Oh, my God, my God," I cried as my legs gave way and I dropped down on the couch.

"I can explain."

"Explain what? How you allowed three boys violate me, rape me?" I screamed, feeling my voice getting weak with each syllable.

"How do you think this makes me feel, I've been living with this guilt my whole life," Raymond said. "I think that was the reason I couldn't get off of drugs. I was trying to bury the guilt and the pain of what I did to you, my little sister," Raymond said as he sobbed.

"Don't you fucking dare blame your drug-infested life for what you did to me. Ever!"

"But I was an addict," he pleaded. "I was sick, sis… I was sick."

"You were supposed to be my brother and protector," I said.

Raymond began to pace as he hit himself in the head with

his fist. "Oh, God, I am so sorry. Please, you have to believe me."

"Do you realize what they did to me, huh? Do you? They not only raped me but they taunted me for hours on end, while you ran off and got high!"

"I didn't know, I didn't know, I didn't know," he cried. "They said they would just touch and feel on you."

"Well, they did a lot more than that and unfortunately for me," I said. "You were too busy getting high to give a shit."

"I'm sorry."

"That you are, a sorry ass excuse for a man. Get the hell out!" I yelled.

"Please, sis, I'm begging you,.."

"Begging me for what, forgiveness? No, I don't think I can forgive you for this one. I don't have anymore forgiveness in my heart for you. So save your apologies for someone who gives a damn, because I don't anymore," I said as I turned to walk out of the room.

"Wait," Raymond said.

"I said to GET OUT!" I yelled one last time as I turned, took two steps toward Raymond, and swung and hit him with three quick blows to the chest.

"Get out! Get out! Get out!" My screams quickly turned to sobs.

Raymond quickly got the hint as he backed away from me and scurried out the door.

I slammed the door behind him and fell to the floor.

I cried, feeling the pain of my brother and his betrayal. I cried until I had no more tears to shed.

45 · CRAZIER THINGS HAVE HAPPENED

MY HEART WAS STILL heavy from the news Raymond had laid on me. It had been a week and since then he had called too many times to count. I couldn't bring myself to forgive him, not right then, not soon, maybe not ever. I felt a tremendous amount of betrayal on so many levels. I was the one who stood by him when people turned their backs. I was the one who pulled him up and that horrible revelation is what I got out of it.

Besides my heavy heart I still wasn't feeling one hundred percent so I decided to go get a check-up before I headed to the Big Apple. I honestly couldn't remember the last time I'd had a full physical. I once read in a magazine that people do a better job at maintaining their cars than their bodies. Crazy but true, and we wonder why diabetes and heart disease are the number one killers today. So with those statistics on my mind I decided to call my doctor and make an appointment for a full-body workup, from head to toe.

My doctor was downtown, Michigan Avenue to be exact. It was a Monday and seeing that my appointment was at 3pm in the afternoon, I opted to take public transportation. No need to get stuck in downtown rush hour traffic if I didn't have to. So I hurried down the street to catch the Number 3 train downtown. I always liked the train, even though I had gotten in the habit of driving to work every day.

I got off the train and headed down Michigan as I window-shopped. I was about forty-five minutes early for my appointment so I decided to peek into Bloomingdales for a minute. I headed through the accessories department, passed by the men's section, and headed up the escalators to the women's shoe section. You never need an excuse to browse for shoes (or in my case, to buy them).

After I accumulated three pairs of Jimmy Choo's, I pranced around like I was Cindy Crawford in her modeling days before heading to the cashier to purchase a pair that would have been a sin to leave behind. I stopped dead in my tracks when I looked up to see Alana doing the exact same thing. My stomach flipped upon seeing her; I wasn't sure if she had seen me, but by her body language I thought she hadn't. I stepped to the side, hiding my body behind a shoe rack, hoping not to make eye contact with her, but we were too close to each other for me to prevent our chance meeting. Although I was not ready to see Alana, nor talk to her, there is that famous saying: There's no time like the present. I figured, what the hell, I was bound to run into her sooner or later.

I walked a few more feet toward Alana as the movement of my body caught her attention, forcing her to look up. We locked eyes and held a stare before she slowly revealed a sly grin. I was silent, not really knowing what to say to her. This was my first time seeing her since our court date. So there we were, face to face, the woman I had had an affair with, who stole my fiancé right out from under me. I told myself to be calm, civil; we were in a public place so I didn't want to draw any attention.

"Hello, Kai," Alana said as she walked a few more steps toward me.

I glanced a few feet behind her to see Riley playing with a pair of shoes on the floor, then back at Alana.

"Hey," I said, with a cold tone.

"So how are you?" she asked.

"Please, like you care," I said.

Alana shrugged her shoulders. "Okay, I don't."

"Exactly," I said, "because you only care about your damn self."

There was another pause, a strained awkwardness. I thought about just walking away, but for some reason I couldn't.

"Listen, Kai, it's unfortunate what happened, but I think everything turned out for the best."

"The best?" I laughed. "You call what happened 'for the best'"?

Alana thought for a moment. "Yes, I do."

"Oh, cut the bullshit, Alana," I said. "I trusted you and you deceived me."

"Wow, that's funny," she retorted. "I mean, coming from the one who deceived her man and all."

I had to laugh at Alana's comeback. "Right, I guess you will always have that one piece of ammunition to use on me for the rest of your life."

"Like I always say, 'Why waste a good shot?'"

"Especially when it's a cheap one," I said.

"Whatever, Kai," Alana said, "It's been a pleasure, but I should go."

I wasn't totally up to talking any more, but I had to do one thing for myself, for the closure that would put my mind at peace and assist me in moving on. "I just have one question, you know, before you have to go that is."

Alana turned back around and just looked at me.

"Why did you set me up like you did? Not only that, you betrayed me, manipulated our intimate relationship, all so you could be with Todd. Was it really that important to you?"

"You'll never understand," she replied.

"Try me," I said, "because at this point, Alana, it really doesn't matter, now does it?"

Alana took a few steps closer to me. "You're right, it doesn't matter. Bottom line, you can never give Todd what he wants and that's a child."

Her words sent a burning sensation through my soul. I wanted to react but I kept it together. She wasn't worth it, not anymore. "You know, Alana, there's more to life than kids".

"Of course there is," she said, "but children are a big part of it, especially when it comes to Todd. Besides, he gets me and I get him, it was always meant for us to be together, and you can't mess with destiny."

"I wouldn't call how you stole Todd from me 'destiny, I'm thinking more down right dirty."

"Call it what you want, Kai, I really don't care," Alana replied. "If you're done with your questions I really should go."

She turned to leave. I let her get a few feet away. "Was there even a Tiffany on the road when you were modeling?"

Alana stopped, turned to face me, then smiled. "Of course not, I made her up, she never even existed."

"You are one selfish bitch, you know that? I can't believe I allowed you to take advantage of my vulnerability and manipulate the whole situation for your benefit, not caring about anyone but yourself," I said.

"You act like you had nothing to do with this," Alana said. "Well, newsflash, it takes two to tango. I may have swayed you into this relationship, but you had every right to stop it before it got too far, and you just chose not to. You're just all pissy 'cause it blew up in your perfect little face. Well, I'm not the one to cry to, Kai. Save it for someone who gives a damn."

"Don't try to twist this Alana," I said. "You knew what you were doing. You may have won this battle but you're going to lose the war. And I think you know that, too, but your ego won't let you see it. Todd is only with you because you manipulated a situation and trapped him, and he thinks he's doing the right thing by being with you, but let's just be clear, it won't last, and I will bet my life on it."

"Well, I'm sorry you feel that way, Kai. I guess I can scratch you off the guest list for our wedding."

"Don't worry about my feelings, Alana," I replied. "Just worry about being discovered as the traitorous bitch that you are. Todd will eventually see right through you, just like I have, and you'll find yourself alone."

"You mean like you are?" she scoffed.

"I won't be for long," I assured her, "because, unlike you, I don't need to lie and manipulate a man into my life, especially if it means sleeping with his best friend. Now, I'm the one who needs to go."

I turned and walked away, not giving Alana the time to reply to my face. I heard her say a few words but I had already tuned her out. I felt good. I had my closure – and a great pair of Jimmy Choo shoes, to boot."

•

I arrived at my doctor's office with a few minutes to spare. I figured I could use the time to do some high-tech Spring cleaning. So I pulled out my cell phone and quickly erased all of Alana's contact information, and while I was at it I did the same for Todd's. Some people would call me bitter, but I call it a fresh start. I threw my phone back into my purse as I waited for the nurse to call me in. I was a little nervous since I had not had a physical since 1852, or so it seemed – but I was generally pretty healthy. I continued to tell myself that as I waited.

Finally the nurse came and got me. She was a nice and very soft-spoken woman who quickly took my height, weight, and blood pressure. She then gave me a small cup and I excused myself to the bathroom. I always hated the whole peeing in the cup thing, because it never failed that when you needed to pee, it never happened. I sat in the bathroom for fifteen minutes before producing a sample for the lab to analyze. What we go through for a physical!

Dr. Matilda Rosenberg entered, a small woman in stature with a big personality. Her vibrant energy always made me smile and right then I needed that.

Dr. Rosenberg studied my chart as she slowly shut the door behind her, then closed the manila folder and looked up at me with a big smile.

"Long time no see, Kai!" she said as she walked over to me. She then put my chart on the table and placed both of her hands in the pockets of her white lab coat.

"Yeah, I've been kinda busy," I said.

"I see, but not as busy as you're about to be."

I looked at Dr. Rosenberg, not totally understanding what she was talking about. "What do you mean?"

The doctor pulled her hands out of her pockets, and threw them up in the air to punctuate her next statement. "Well, Kai, you may not believe this, but you're pregnant."

"I'm what?" I exclaimed.

"Pregnant."

"Pregnant? But I thought?"

"You couldn't get pregnant? Well, there was a possibility, but there was also a small percentage that you could too. So Congratulations! Consider it a blessing from God."

As Dr. Rosenberg stood in front of me displaying a smile that would light up the state of Illinois, my world as I knew it stopped spinning. Never in a million years had I thought I would ever get pregnant. But then again, I thought, crazier things have happened.

Okay, time to show Alana and Todd what I was working with!

THE END